Resounding Praise for
Child of Silence . . .

"A tense and tidy thriller. . . . Padgett knows how to tell a story well and, in Bo Bradley, has created an engagingly eccentric heroine."

—**San Diego Union-Tribune**

* * *

"Truly exceptional . . . Padgett gets high marks for originality and style. She creates fresh, fascinating characters and situations . . . and fast-moving suspense to keep one reading very, very late into the night."

—**Mystery News**

* * *

"A welcome addition to the mystery categories . . . unique to the genre."

—**United Press International**

* * *

"Abigail Padgett's first novel contains a fascinating blend of mystery, mysticism, and near madness. Her evocative prose, likable and believable protagonist, and keen psychological insight add up to an impressive debut."

—**Marcia Muller, author of**
Pennies on a Dead Woman's Eyes

more. . .

"Padgett's debut stands out for Bo's memorable battles with her tormenting gifts (heightened perceptions, intuitions, delusions). Given the manic-depressive bent of detectives ever since Sherlock Holmes, why hasn't anybody thought of all this before?"

—*Kirkus Reviews*

* * *

"Keeps you reading until the very end."

—*Tribune Daily News*
(San Gabriel, CA)

* * *

"Realistically drawn characters and a fast-paced plot, but what makes it exceptional is the slant that the manic-depression angle puts on the writing itself."

—*Mostly Murder*

* * *

"Memorable . . . a taut, suspenseful mystery . . . set against a Tony Hillerman-like backdrop of desert scenery and native American culture."

—*Roanoke Times & World-News*

* * *

"Powerful and suspenseful."

—*Mystery and Detective Monthly*

ABIGAIL PADGETT

CHILD OF SILENCE

THE MYSTERIOUS PRESS

Published by Warner Books

A Time Warner Company

Enjoy lively book discussions online with CompuServe. To become a member of CompuServe call 1-800-848-8199 and ask for the Time Warner Trade Publishing forum. (Current members GO:TWEP.)

For Ruth Cavin
And in memory of Tarot D.

Quoted lines of the Paiute chant by Wovoka are used by permission of the Bear Tribe Publishing Company in cooperation with The Draco Foundation and are taken from Evelyn Eaton's "Snowy Earth Comes Gliding" © 1974 by The Draco Foundation.

MYSTERIOUS PRESS EDITION

Cover design by Jackie Merri Meyer
Cover illustration by Terrence Cummings

The Mysterious Press name and logo are trademarks of Warner Books, Inc.

 Mysterious Press books are published by
Warner Books, Inc.
1271 Avenue of the Americas
New York, NY 10020

 A Time Warner Company

Printed in the United States of America

Originally published in hardcover by The Mysterious Press.
First Printed in Paperback: February, 1994
10 9 8 7 6 5 4 3 2 1

Acknowledgments

To writers Mary Austin and Evelyn Eaton, who at different times loved and wrote about a lost desert valley in California and its native people, the Paiute.

To Dr. Dennis Agallianos of Vermont's Brattleboro Retreat—gentleman and wisest of shrinks—for psychiatric technical advice.

To Dr. Tom Humphries of the San Diego Community College District for technical advice on hearing impairment.

To Louise Warner, my typist and first fan, who begged me not to kill one of the characters.

And to my agent, Sandra Dijkstra, and editor, Sara Ann Freed.

1

3:00 A.M. Fog

Wisps of fog drifting through the open balcony doors of Bo Bradley's San Diego beach apartment wafted aimlessly and then evaporated. But not before settling damply on her unruly mane of silvery auburn hair. And not before capturing the attention of an almond-shaped structure called the amygdala, nestled deep within Bo's brain.

More highly evolved in dogs than in people, the amygdala responds to scent. In the more imaginative, it can create whole movies out of a whiff of yeast muffin or a hint of perfume. And prone toward the manic end of a manic-depressive disorder, Bo Bradley was never short of imagination, even in sleep.

Irritated, she stretched her lanky forty-year-old frame beneath the Black Watch plaid sheets she'd found on sale at a linen outlet just last week. She pulled the edge of the top sheet over her nose. Too late. Images called by the scent of fog from inaccessible memory crowded into other landscapes and became mutations. Bo began to dream.

It was the old cottage at Chequesset Neck on Cape Cod

Bay where she'd gone every summer as a child. The salt-breezy cottage with its ship's-prow porch where her grandmother told stories of Billingsgate sea witches and Gypsy fortune-tellers. Except in the dream the cottage was in ruins, its clapboard roof fallen in on hollow rooms strewn with broken glass.

There was no one in the ravaged rooms but her sister, Laurie, screaming that eerie, croaking scream of hers. A child-Laurie, screaming alone in the ruined cottage. And she was wearing the dress. Gray velvet with the Carrickmacross lace collar that had belonged to their grandmother. The dress Laurie had really worn at twenty. The dress she would wear forever.

Bo wakened to the booming of her own heart and the echo of a scream. Her throat hurt. The scream, she assumed, must have originated there.

"Here we go again," she muttered at a digital clock radio greenly promoting the fact that it was the middle of the night and Friday as well. "I'm not up for this. I'm really not."

It was Laurie again. Or the memory of Laurie. Or guilt over Laurie. Or some damn thing. Whatever. But after twelve years Bo knew what to do. Twelve years after Laurie's body had been found in a rest area off the New York Thruway with a garden hose running from the exhaust pipe of her car through the driver's-side window, Bo knew exactly what to do. Her all-time favorite shrink, the inimitable Dr. Lois Bittner, had told her how to manage these "occurrences."

"Immediate exercise!" the wiry little woman yelped cheerfully, as if exercise were the equivalent of a quarter pound of fudge—something to *brighten* over. "Take control! Increase your heart rate. Pump up your body. Don't let the mood pull you into tangential thinking. Remember, der iss *nutting* but reality.''

Lois Bittner, Bo remembered fondly, invariably lapsed into an accent you couldn't cut with an industrial-strength laser when she waxed enthusiastic. Which was often.

Pulling paint-smudged sweats over a tattered old T-shirt of Mark's she sometimes slept in, Bo fumbled for her Nikes under the bed and took a deep breath. Her grandmother would have sniffed at Dr. Bittner.

''It's the sight,'' Bridget Mairead O'Reilly explained to her granddaughter. ''A gift. Those as has it, well . . . they seem to *know* things, to *see* things as others can't.''

It would be fun, Bo thought, to lock the two matriarchs in a room and let *them* fight over where to draw the line between intuition and madness. The Irish Catholic grandmother and the German Jewish psychiatrist. Maybe then she could get some sleep. Too bad they were both dead.

In her basket on the floor near an easel, Bo's elderly fox terrier, Mildred, blinked groggily and attempted to wag her stub of a tail.

''Never mind,'' Bo reassured the dog. ''It's the middle of the night. You don't have to get up. I'm fine.''

Mildred sighed and allowed her white fur eyelids to close. On the easel an egg-tempera pictograph of a bighorn sheep appeared to do the same. ''Or am I?'' Bo questioned as she opened the door of her apartment to a swirling wall of fog. At this hour it was hard to tell.

Beneath her feet the crooked stone steps that in daylight would angle charmingly toward gull-strewn rocks hissing with foamy breakers were invisible. She felt her way down, holding the railing and fighting a suspicion that familiar paths may not always lead where they always have. What if, unaccountably, the steps just led nowhere? Off into oblivion? Into a black hole? The fog moved in sinuous clumps like a living thing struggling toward some destination of its own.

Warning signals went up. Just little ones, but the snick of their ignition was almost audible. This was it. The thing to watch out for. The acceleration of imagination beyond the boundaries of comfort.

"Cut the crap." Bo admonished several thousand neural synapses inside her skull. "There is *nothing* but reality!"

It usually worked. It and a lot of exercise, a relentlessly healthy diet, and rigorous elimination of stress. What a joke.

Bo laughed, imagining Dr. Bittner's probable response to her current job as a child abuse investigator for San Diego County's Juvenile Court. If there were a more stress-ridden, emotionally wracking form of employment on earth, Bo couldn't name it. Bittner would have calves, Bo knew. Whole litters of them! But Lois Bittner was dead. And the job paid Bo's rent, as long as she didn't let it get to her.

And all else failing, there was always the damned lithium. She'd had to take it before, more than once; she'd do it again when the inevitable necessity arose.

"But I'd rather not," Bo sang determinedly into the fog as her feet found the narrow path to the Ocean Beach Pier. The last time she'd had to take the famous salts to calm her racing mind, her supervisor at work, the American Gothic Madge Aldenhoven, complimented her on her sudden "maturity." Chronic ringworm, Bo mused, would be preferable to Madge's brand of maturity. What Madge meant was nothing more than tidy paperwork and blind obedience to the bureaucracy. Bo had never been renowned for tidy paperwork or obedience to anything.

The Ocean Beach Pier loomed whitely out of the fog, promising a good jog. Bo knew every board of the creaking old pier, and could run it blindfolded. The smooth increase in her heart rate was comforting. It would reduce the restlessness, drain the content of the crazy dreams. A little.

A dark heap under a fish-cleaning sink appeared suddenly and turned out to be a pile of kelp. Someone fishing had undoubtedly hauled it up and left it there, its rubbery green leaves browning at the edges. Bo stopped to toss it over the rail. It vanished instantly into the white mist and made no splash when it hit the water. The fog simply swallowed it.

Still, behind the white swirls Bo could swear she felt something happening. Something vague and distant, but nevertheless desperate. Something about Laurie. It made no sense and that, Bo knew, was dangerous.

Her grandmother would have lit a candle and rattled a few rosaries. Bo chose instead to increase the pace of her jog and wondered idly if she'd inadvertently propel herself over the rail at the end of the pier and vanish in fog, like the kelp.

The weird feeling wasn't going away.

A gong buoy beyond the twin breakwaters to her right clanged in the manner relished by Victorian poets. Eerie and prophetic. Bo couldn't see the buoy but knew its shape—a small blue Eiffel Tower lurching in the swells.

"Oh, shut up," she told it.

At the end of the pier she leaned on the railing and breathed fog. Except for the buoy there was no sound. Her throat still hurt and numerous small headaches twitched sporadically behind her eyes. A dawning awareness that she might be physically sick rose like a warm, pink sun. Sore throat and headache? Bingo!

"I'm not getting manic, I'm getting sick," Bo told the pier railing with enthusiasm. "It's the flu!"

And regardless how stuffy, drippy, achy, and miserable it might be, the flu was a piece of cake compared to that other alternative. Hands down.

On the return jog Bo forced her attention into the labyrinth of the mundane with its comforting boredom. She'd try to catch another three hours of sleep and then maybe get to the office early. She couldn't stay home; she'd used all of her sick days in pursuit of her current fascination—the primitive paintings.

A bit of rock at a museum exhibit had started it. Just a meaningless spiral-shaped squiggle etched on a rock many centuries before the first white explorer would claim the land for condos and shopping malls. Bo had felt the bit of rock, the inexplicable spiral on its surface, pulling at her. Had felt some antediluvian hand arching in her own fingers. The need to create images, the artist's need. She welcomed it, familiar as her first tin tray of watercolors. Art was the only language she knew that could be understood on either side of the line marked "sanity."

"Where is this from?" she asked, dragging the museum docent to the display case. "Were these done by Anasazi People, or does anybody know? Are there any more drawings? How do I get there?"

The docent had to pull a file from a dusty cabinet.

"... Mojave desert ... a valley in the Coso Range, now part of the China Lake Naval Air Station. It's about five hours north of here, up toward Death Valley," the woman explained. "Nothing is known of the people who left the drawings. Tribes now living in the region do not regard the creators of the drawings as ancestors, and refer to them merely as 'the old ones' ..."

Bo spent two days doodling spirals on interoffice memos before capitulating to the fascination. A fictitious bout of bronchitis bought her a four-day weekend. Plenty of time for exploring a silent desert canyon whose walls were galleries of forgotten art. Spellbound, Bo longed to bring the images out of silence, give them new life on her own canvases. She wished she didn't have to work. She wished she could make a living with her painting.

"But so what?" she commented to one of San Diego's homeless, irritably trying to sleep on a fishing bench. "I mean, it could be worse, right?"

"Right, lady," the man muttered dismally. "It could be worse, like if you don't get the hell outta here!"

Bo chose not to explain the public nature of the pier and her right to be there despite fog and wee hours.

It was going to be okay. She'd go to work, stay in the office all day, finish up the paperwork trailing the ten cases she'd investigated already this month. Take it easy. It would be a good day. It would be good to have the flu.

Mildred was waiting at the door when Bo returned, a bundle of leaps and wags. Gathering the little dog in her arms, Bo buried her face in comforting, furry warmth.

"Aye, an' there's a banshee after me for sure," she joked as the dog cocked an ear curiously at her brogue.

"It's Caillech Bera a wailin' in the fog."

The reference to the ancient Celtic goddess of death and madness failed to achieve the level of parody Bo had intended. In fact, the words seemed oddly, and quite sanely, true.

2

"The Crow Has Called Me..."
—Arapaho Ghost Dance

Dawn sieved through the leaves of coast live oaks off Wildcat Canyon Road on the Barona Ranch Indian Reservation thirty miles east of San Diego. The light roused mountain jays, quail, and one sluggish crow. The crow swooped erratically to land on the roof of a ramshackle trailer. Its cawing wakened the woman inside.

"What does Little Black Eagle want with an old woman?" Annie Garcia muttered to herself.

At seventy-nine she had little use for spirit-messages, especially before she'd had her coffee. And maybe it wasn't a spirit-message, but just a crow. It was hard to separate the old Paiute ways from modern ways, in her mind. Mostly, she didn't try. Sometimes, she thought she was a girl again, sleeping with her grandmother beneath a blanket of woven rabbit skins in the lonely Sierra reaches beyond Yosemite. Sometimes she only wished she were.

Her body hurt in more places than she could name. She could feel every interstice of bone and bone. Her chest ached; her breath was short. A cry-dance lay not far in the future, and Annie knew it would be for her—the somber Paiute circle-dance around a fire in which her belongings would burn.

But not today.

She forced a gnarled foot to find her shoes beneath the cot—men's Adidas her oldest daughter, Maria Bigger Fox, got for her in a thrift store in El Cajon. The shoes were loose and comfortable for walking. Annie liked to walk.

After a trip to the chemical toilet behind the trailer, she began. It wasn't too far. Just past Maria and Joe's cement-block house, up Wildcat Canyon Road, and onto the dirt track to the old house.

She walked up to the house whenever she could. It reminded her of one she and Charlie rented in Three Rivers years ago when the kids were little and he made some money in the almond groves.

The path looked safe today. The car that somebody parked at the trailhead was gone.

People slept at the old house sometimes. Indian kids with beer who shot guns at the walls. Knots of hungry Mexicans on their way north to work. But almost never a white, like the one with the car.

Leaning against a cottonwood, Annie paused to get her breath in the early-morning damp. Her heart trembled briefly and then resumed a painful thumping she could feel in her knuckles. A spadefoot toad stared at her from its hole in the ditch beside the path. Annie stared back and then kicked a shower of dust and granite pebbles at its bulging head. The toad was so ugly it made her laugh as she struggled uphill.

But the laugh subsided when she saw the house. It was just an adobe shell crumbling amid granite boulders and shrubby manzanitas with their smooth, mahogany-colored limbs. The bullet-pocked walls and gaping windows were as familiar to Annie as her own wide and crumpled face. But something was wrong.

A spirit shook her suddenly and then moved away through the oaks in a shower of tear-shaped acorns that rattled on the licheny boulders. It was too quiet!

There was no sound. No gray squirrels scrabbling among the dry October leaves. No jays screeching in the oaks. No crows swooping and cawing in the whole expanse of ashen sky.

A chill moved up Annie's spine like a hand of feathers under her skin. The spirit had warned her.

"Better go, old woman," she told herself. "Something bad here."

Then she smiled and moved instead toward the house. Not for nothing did her people name her Sees the Dark. Unable to describe the emotion known as fear, Annie knew as second nature the fierce tug of curiosity.

The sweep of her gaze revealed gray clouds moving in layers, a limb of oak, three mossy stone steps, and the hollow doorway of the house. Entering, her nostrils flared at the scent of rot in the place and other, more recent smells. Excrement, vomit, fear.

There was something odd in the murky shadows beneath what remained of the roof. Annie blinked, trying to focus. Something on an old mattress in front of the fireplace, something tied to the mattress with clothesline, its eyes rolled back and white as eggs. Something barely alive.

Annie had been a mother five times. Even in the gloom with her failing eyes she could see what it was. It was a child.

3

"I Scream Because I Am a Bird"
—*Pa-guadal*

Bo awoke with an epic headache and blearily noted an absence of early-morning silence that could only mean one thing. The clock radio, softly cranking out Danny and the Juniors' 1958 hit, "At the Hop," confirmed her worst suspicion. It was 8:15. She'd overslept.

"Shit!" She yelled with an enthusiasm that hurt her throat. Madge Aldenhoven was going to kill her. To make matters worse, every item of clothing she pulled from the closet revealed a heretofore unseen stain, tear, or wrinkle.

"Does this happen to everybody, or just to me?" she asked Mildred. "Do my clothes actually *plot* against me, or am I acting out a subconscious wish to avoid going to work?" The obvious answer made her grin as she pulled on an ancient Irish fisherman's sweater still redolent of the buttered popcorn she'd enjoyed last night during a Pavarotti rerun. The sweater would have been baggy on the stocky tenor; on Bo it resembled a hot-air balloon. The corduroys she found in the back of her closet under a bolt of canvas matched, she noted ruefully, nothing she'd ever owned.

11

What had possessed her to buy red-and-black herringbone? Just looking at the fabric made her feel queasy.

"Madge," she wheezed into the bedside phone after dialing the well-known number, "I'm sick. But I'm coming in anyway. I'll stay at the office and catch up on paperwork. Just dock me an hour. I'll be in."

The supervisor's voice was businesslike.

"If you're really sick, stay home. If you're coming in, you've got a new case—"

"I've *what . . . !*"

Bo flung herself on the unmade bed and reveled in its retained warmth.

"Madge, I've got the flu or something. I can't interview any kids today..."

It was tempting just to drop the bomb, to say, "Madge, you don't know this, but I'm a manic-depressive and if I don't get out from under that grueling job and your ever-present thumb for a while, I may come to work in a jacket with sleeves that tie in back, so give me a break!" So tempting. And so stupid. She'd be out of a job in less time than it would take Aldenhoven to complete the paperwork. Better to play the game.

". . . found the child on the Barona Reservation," Madge was going on, "but it's not an Indian child, so you don't have to worry about dealing with the Indian Child Welfare Council . . ."

"Madge, I'm really sick, but I don't have any sick leave left. I have to come in. Can't you just give the case to somebody else?"

The thought of staying home was immensely appealing. Bo trailed a finger over the open book she'd fallen asleep reading—part of the background research for the primitive paintings. She'd bought the book near Lone Pine when she'd gone up into the high desert to photograph the mysterious rock drawings left there by long-vanished artists.

"I scream because I am a bird," sang a line of Paiute chant from the page. "The boy will rise up."

Bo wished for the three-millionth time that she could make a living with her art. The social work degree that qualified her as an investigator had been earned when it had not occurred to her that she might someday have to support herself. The Paiute chant shimmered curiously on its page as Bo blinked and felt her brow for fever. That eerie, compelling feeling was back. Something happening, something already in progress.

"It's an easy one," the supervisor continued persuasively. "An NPG. You can probably transfer it out today."

A "no parent or guardian." Bo brightened. NPGs were the cases most coveted by the overworked investigators. Abandoned children. There was nothing to investigate. The court automatically had jurisdiction, and the Department of Social Services automatically got custody. The kids automatically went straight to foster homes. No hearings, no trials. No fuss, no muss. A minimum of paperwork, finished in a day.

"Okay, okay," she sighed. "I'll take it."

She hadn't really paid any attention to Madge's description of the case, but NPGs were easy. Now she wouldn't have to work on Saturday. She could paint all weekend. Heaven!

After dropping Mildred with a retired neighbor whose monthly Social Security allotment Bo supplemented with dog-sitting fees, she eased her threadbare BMW onto the freeway. The fog was still thick and most of the cars heading inland had their lights on. The effect was disorienting. Hazy, bulbous globs of light emerging and disappearing in layers of mist. She felt dizzy, hypnotized.

"Danger," she pronounced warily. And she didn't mean the traffic.

"There is nothing but reality," she reminded herself. Whatever that was.

And unfortunately it was probably Madge Aldenhoven. All the Madges of the world who made all the rules of the world and then insisted that everybody else observe them. Whether they made any sense or not. Except Madge hadn't been abusive or dictatorial. In fact, she'd been almost nice. And totally out of character.

It dawned on Bo that Madge must be up to something. It was too late to care. She'd find out soon enough.

Her office mate, Estrella Benedict, was still in when Bo arrived and switched on the desk lamp.

"Madre de dios!" the well-dressed Latina yelped. "What did *you* do last night? Drink pulque till dawn in some Tijuana dive? You look like parrot puke and you're an hour late."

Bo couldn't help envisioning a hung-over parrot with an ice pack, heaving over a tiny toilet in the corner of a bird cage strewn with tiny, empty bottles. The parrot's eyes would have Xs in them.

"Thanks, Es." Bo grinned. "I think I'm getting the flu. What's pool-kay?"

"Fermented cactus juice. Tastes like rotten lawn clippings and feels like mucus. Distilled, it becomes tequila. But they always leave a worm in the bottle to remind you where it came from. I hear you got a new case."

Bo nodded at the new case file on her desk, "JOHNNY DOE" penned across the edge in thick black marker. "Madge seemed to want me to handle it. It's just an NPG."

A flicker of concern crossed Estrella's face and then vanished.

"What is it?" Bo asked in the next second. She missed

nothing. Not the slightest nuance of human expression. It was "the gift of the curse," as Lois Bittner had put it. The heightened acuity that in a manic state could become distorted and bizarre, but was always, *always* there. It was the reason so many manic-depressives were writers, artists, poets, composers—that ever-present sensitivity to nuance. It was the reason Bo could tell instantly when people were lying. It could also be a pain in the neck.

"You'd better read the case before you kick off your shoes and order pizza," Estrella replied. "And for starters, look who's taken *personal* charge of it over at St. Mary's."

Bo pushed aside several unruly stacks of files, memos, and assorted paper to make space atop her desk, and opened the Johnny Doe file to its face-sheet.

"Andrew LaMarche! Why? He called it in himself at seven this morning. What's Dr. Andrew LaMarche, world-renowned hotshot, doing at work at seven in the morning and taking the time to report cases to Child Protective Services like any other peon?"

"I don't know why he chose to call it in," Estrella sighed, "but he's at work getting ready to crucify the department at the Martinelli review. Don't you remember? It's today."

"I forgot," Bo murmured.

There was a moment of silence, the one invariably observed by child abuse workers at the mention of a case in which a child has been murdered.

And Jennifer Martinelli, all of seven years old, had been murdered. Her mother's crystal-meth-abusing boyfriend threw the child across the living room and onto the handlebars of the motorcycle he'd parked there. Four broken ribs and a shattered breastbone all punctured the little girl's lungs.

Angela Reavey, the reunification worker who'd believed Christina Martinelli when she said Rob Pickthall would never come near Jennifer again, had recommended to the court that Jennifer be returned to her mother. Only three days before her death Jennifer had left her foster home and rejoined Christina.

Angela Reavey wouldn't be at the case review called by Dr. LaMarche at St. Mary's Hospital for Children this morning. She'd be home in bed, heavily sedated, unable to cry anymore. Andrew LaMarche, international authority on child abuse, would vent his rage at San Diego County's Child Protective Services and the San Diego County Juvenile Court without her. There would be reporters from every major newspaper in California as well as several of the national media, and a collection of tight-lipped county officials. There would be nobody who'd ever laid eyes on Jennifer Martinelli. It would not be a good day to chat with Andrew LaMarche about an abandoned child.

The sound of shallow nasal breathing alerted Bo to the presence of Madge Aldenhoven hehind her.

"Bo? I want you to take special care with this case."

The veteran supervisor looked, as usual, as if she were expecting to lunch with the Queen Mother. Real pearls. A blue silk shirtwaist that accented her eyes. It had puzzled Bo the entire two years of her job with CPS. Madge, the only one of them who never went out of the building, was the only one who dressed to the teeth every day.

"No kidding." Bo grimaced. "You didn't tell me LaMarche was handling this."

"Yes," Madge Aldenhoven went on as if Bo had casually mentioned the fact that Halloween was just around the corner. "He'll be tearing into the department at the Martinelli review right now. Give it your best. We need to look good."

"In case you hadn't noticed," Bo said, narrowing her wide green eyes to slits, "looking good wasn't a big priority for me today."

"You know what I mean," Madge snapped, tucking a Bic pen through her swan-white hair. "Just do it."

And Bo did know. Her court reports, if frequently late, were unerringly full of precisely the information needed by the juvenile judges to determine a child's fate. Bo could assess a situation in minutes. She knew who was lying, who was on drugs, who was covering up a propensity for abusing or molesting children. At court they called her Mandrake the Magician. But nobody, except Estrella, knew why.

To have Bo Bradley investigate a case meant it would be done right. And everybody in the system, including Andrew LaMarche, knew it.

The case file held a fact-sheet blank except for the name of the reporting party, the doctor himself. Literally nothing was known about the child whose case Bo was supposed to investigate.

Behind the face-sheet were reports faxed over from the San Diego County Sheriff's Department and from the ambulance service.

"Responded to call from ANNIE GARCIA, 79, a Paiute Indian living with her daughter and son-in-law, MARIA AND JOSEPH BIGGER FOX, on the Barona Indian Reservation," Sheriff's Deputy John Greenlea had printed correctly. "GARCIA reported finding an abandoned Caucasian male child in a deserted building on the reservation at about 5:30 A.M. . . ."

The paramedic's report was more specific.

"Found male Caucasian child who had been tied to a mattress with clothesline. The child's breath smelled of urea. Suspect dehydration. The body was clammy and the pulse weak and rapid. Suspect shock. Child breathing. No endotracheal airway needed. Vomitus and very fluid feces dried on child's clothing and the mattress. Oxygen and 2.5 glucose solution administered IV in ambulance. Child unconscious, secured to gurney. Arrive St. Mary's ER 6:41 A.M.''

A strange one.

A shiver rippled along Bo's shoulders and trembled in her hands. That odd feeling again. Something creepy about this case!

"No big deal," she told herself philosophically as she headed out the office door. "Just get to St. Mary's while LaMarche is still in the Martinelli review, see the kid, and get out of there." No big deal.

4

The Slaughter of the Innocent

The conference room was jammed with reporters, most of them young. They bit the ends of pens provided by the hospital and tried to look appropriately shocked without allowing the full impact of the report to sink in.

The hospital's public relations director finished a subdued and clinical description of Jennifer Martinelli's final moments with gasp-producing information.

"Although the child was pronounced dead on arrival at this hospital at 10:23 Thursday night, the San Diego County Medical Examiner's report indicates that the time of death was actually some three hours earlier." Here he looked somberly at the crowd. "Jennifer lay dead on her mother's living room floor for over two hours before anyone bothered to wonder why she wasn't moving."

Perfect.

No one in the room was breathing.

Andrew LaMarche had written the PR man's presentation himself only an hour ago. It was the lead-in for his own remarks.

19

The four representatives of the Department of Social Services and the three Juvenile Court attorneys looked intently everywhere except at Dr. Andrew LaMarche as he replaced the PR man at the podium.

"I attended Jennifer Martinelli when she was brought to St. Mary's the first time, a month ago. She was suffering from lacerations on her face, neck, arms, and legs—everywhere, in fact, that her body wasn't protected by clothing. Her mother's live-in boyfriend had chosen tó punish her for breaking a piece of his drug paraphernalia by beating her violently with an electrical cord."

In a mirror at the far end of the conference room Andrew LaMarche saw himself reflected, the full-spectrum TV camera lights shimmering off his graying mustache and white lab coat. The look was right. Avenging angel. Tight-lipped spokesman for good.

A facade, but an effective one.

Practically no one knew the man behind it.

"At that time," he went on, "I told Jennifer's Child *Protective* Services worker, Ms. Angela Reavey..." He paused to allow the irony of the emphasized word to sink in, "that until the perpetrator was dead or imprisoned and the mother had completed alcohol detoxification and at least six months of alcoholism treatment, Jennifer should not be allowed near these . . . people."

The pause made clear that his personal choice of nouns would have been more like "vermin." Several of the reporters nodded unconsciously.

"But as Ms. Reavey has chosen not to be present at this inquiry, we'll have to rely on other representatives of the Department of Social Services for an explanation of *why* this child was returned to killers within a month. Gentlemen?"

Andrew LaMarche knew perfectly well that no one from DSS could say a word about this or any other case, even if they had guns at their heads. The law was abundantly clear. The confidentiality of DSS and Juvenile Court records was so tight God couldn't crack it. And it always made the department look bad—as if it were deliberately hiding its incompetence.

One of the DSS people made vague noises about "deep regret" and "a thorough investigation of the case's handling." Some of the reporters sneered openly. All of them copied the quotes directly onto notepads. San Diego County's Department of Social Services would look like a drooling idiot in tonight's papers.

It was a step.

It wouldn't save Jennifer Martinelli, but it might save another one, like the strange boy brought in this morning, abandoned in some mountain shack. That one appeared to be retarded—a high risk for abuse. That one or the next. LaMarche didn't care. He just fought for them, fought against a bureaucracy that seemed to value a parent's right to torture offspring over a child's right to grow up unscarred. He would never understand why a genetic relationship should give anyone the right to commit crimes for which in other circumstances they would be imprisoned or put to death.

"Thank you all for coming," he intoned, unclipping the tiny microphone from a watered silk tie bought in Paris.

"The old fag's really pissed over this one!" a young reporter in faded jeans muttered to a companion within earshot of the doctor as the crowd filed out.

"You're damn right," LaMarche whispered to himself.

That everybody assumed his impeccable grooming meant he was gay didn't bother him at all. That, and the French accent he couldn't suppress when he was angry, only added to the mystique he'd spent years refining. The renegade doctor. The eccentric. Champion of the helpless. Brilliant weirdo.

A gust of air rattled the typed speech still in his hand and swept up his lab coat like a cape as he exited by a side door. The presentation, Andrew LaMarche felt, had been flawless.

5

Nurse Sailboat

The third-floor charge nurse on duty at St. Mary's was new—not one of the regulars Bo had come to know during frequent visits there required by her job. Visits in which the most bizarre questions became commonplace.

"Can you tell me what room you were in when Daddy kicked your tummy?"

"When did Aunt Margaret make you eat the cat's food? Was it daytime or nighttime?"

The Juvenile Court demanded specific information. Reports prepared by the investigators were accepted as "clear and convincing" proof of wrongdoing. Often in the absence of witnesses, a typed report alone stood between a child and further abuse, perhaps death.

It had taken Bo months to construct the protective shell that lay between every child abuse investigator and the fits of rage, sleepless nights, and nervous exhaustion that went with the job.

She could sit on the floor and chat calmly with three-year-olds about unusual sexual practices. She could photograph burns left by lit cigarettes on the genitals of babies. She could even observe an occasional autopsy without popping Valium or gaining fifty pounds of buffering flesh as so many of her peers did.

Years of psychiatric treatment notwithstanding, she really lay the credit for her equanimity at the feet of Bach—that hypnotic sanity of sound her violinist mother had taught her to love. The music that her sister, Laurie, had never been able to hear. She hummed the opening bars of "Jesu, Joy of Man's Desiring" as the charge nurse looked at her expectantly.

"Yes?"

Bo resisted the impulse to reply "No," and remembered that she hadn't clipped on the requisite Child Protective Services badge with which she could gain entrance practically anywhere. She found it in her purse between her wallet and a flattened pack of Gauloises.

"I need to see a Johnny Doe brought in this morning from the Barona Reservation," she explained, snapping the badge to her sweater. There was something about the pink-cheeked blonde Bo found unnerving.

"We're taking good care of the little guy," the nurse cooed. "He's in room 323."

"I think I've got the flu," Bo mentioned. She scanned the nurses' station for information that might explain the unpleasant impression. "I'll need a gown and a mask and I won't get too close. But I have to see him."

"Of course," the nurse sang and pulled a clean gown and mask from a closet. "I'm afraid this little one lacks some of the blessings we all take for granted, poor thing. He may be severely retarded."

Blessings? Bo's swift gaze pounced on the answer. Beside the intercom was a hard-back copy of something titled *Shepherdology: A Map for Your Life*. The book's jacket depicted a sailboat aground in the pages of a Bible. The day was running true to form. At this rate, Bo predicted, she could expect to be hijacked to La Paz by extraterrestrials in Elvis costumes before noon.

"Have you read any of Dr. Hinckle's work?" the nurse asked.

"Uh, no. Is he a medical doctor or a Ph.D.?"

Or a charlatan with one hand in the frightened psyches of people like you and the other in a numbered Swiss bank account?

Laurie had fallen in with one of these when she was in college. A suave phony with a mail-order ministerial degree. He'd convinced the impressionable young woman she didn't need to take the medication prescribed by her psychiatrist for depression. She only needed to give him every cent she had, and trust in God. Bo dreamed of what she would do if she ever ran across the guy.

"Oh, Dr. Hinckle's just marvelous!" the nurse gushed. "Why don't you let me lend you one of his books? I've got all of them . . ."

"No, really, I never have time to read," Bo lied. "Is 323 this way?"

She coughed dramatically behind the surgical mask to keep the nurse at a distance and walked toward the kid's room while struggling into the gown. It turned out to be a size meant for juvenile surgical patients. Over her bulky sweater the duckling-and-bunny-imprinted garment served the purpose of a straitjacket. She looked, she thought, like a medical journal ad for a major tranquilizer.

The kid on the bed thought so too. A small but refreshingly sardonic smile crossed his pale lips as he watched her enter the room. He was white as a cave fish and his hair looked like a thatch of rusty steel wool. But the body beneath his hospital gown was sturdy, fleshed-out. Nobody had starved this kid, and he bore none of the telltale scars, bruises, and body tremors of abuse. Under feathery lashes his huge tan eyes betrayed fear, but something else as well. A spark, bright as the sun on desert quartz. In Bo's experience that spark was the only thing that mattered in the end. Still, she wasn't sure.

"Hi." Bo smiled uselessly behind the mask. "My name's Bo, like a clown!"

Kids always grinned at that, but this one merely looked at her, watched her intently. Bo found the boy's look strangely familiar, but couldn't identify it. She noticed the bright plaid restraint vest over the boy's chest. Its ties, Bo knew from her own experience, were secured to the bed frame out of the boy's reach.

"Why the restraints?" she asked Nurse Sailboat, who was hovering behind and reeking of a perfume that intensified Bo's wooziness. The whole room seemed to be humming now. A sense of immediacy, of compelling importance. But without reference in any rational framework. Objects, the boy himself, appeared to shimmer.

Oh shit! This is how it begins. Don't let it.

"He kept flapping his little hands and trying to get out of bed," Sailboat replied softly. "Of course he's upset, poor thing."

Bo wrapped a hand over the cool metal footboard of the boy's bed to regain her equilibrium. The rational course would be simply to document the boy's current condition, return the case file to Madge, and drive straight to the university drop-in psychiatric clinic. That sudden awareness of objects in a room, of the hidden personalities possessed by items of furniture, and the inchoate messages beamed by the play of light on surfaces—these Bo recognized for what they were. The first groundswells of mania.

But the intensity of the boy's odd eyes cut through the illusion and gleamed at Bo. Reached out. Touched her. A

light, a presence. She could no more walk away from it than
she could stop breathing. It was her talisman, that gleam.
Her own source of strength and endurance. It was intelligence! She was sure. She'd know it anywhere.

"Didn't you say you suspect severe retardation?" she
asked without breaking eye contact with the child. Everything in the room had a halo and the hum continued, but she
ignored it.

Sailboat stroked the boy's incredibly thick, wiry hair and
crooned, "Johnny doesn't talk, doesn't understand anything. Do you, Johnny?"

The child continued to stare at Bo. His pale golden eyes
with their sorrel irises spoke volumes. But volumes of
what?

Sailboat went on. "All he can do is flap his hands. We'll
know more when the neurological workup comes back."

Flaps his hands. Bo steadied herself and watched the
boy's right hand. It was "flapping" for sure, but the flap
wasn't random. He'd curled the three middle fingers inward
toward his palm, extending his thumb and pinky. At first Bo
thought he was finger-spelling the letter Y. But the hand
jerked sideways, thumb pointing down toward his mouth. It
was a gesture common to college students, and beer drink-
ers in general.

"I think he wants a beer," Bo gasped.

The humming subsided. The shimmers faded to haze.
What the hell is going on?

A sense of mystery, and of mission, flooded Bo's awareness.
The manicky delusion that she had been brought to this
place by magical forces was at once ludicrous and impossible to shake.

"Don't be silly," Sailboat said professionally.

Bo pulled her mask off. The boy's condition seemed
obvious, but she had to be sure.

"Bo," she pronounced soundlessly, pointing to herself.

"I'm afraid you'll have to keep the mask on. You said you had the flu—"

"No, no. He has to see my face."

Moving to the bedside table, Bo poured water into a plastic cup from a pitcher. Making the beer-drinking gesture with one hand, she handed the cup to the boy. He took a sip and then threw the cup on the floor, his eyes never leaving hers.

She was sure!

"See, he's not thirsty," the nurse sighed. "Now I'll have to call housekeeping to clean this up. Be careful you don't breathe on him."

Bo knew the boy wasn't thirsty. He couldn't be thirsty with a half gallon of nutrient-enriched sugar-water dripping into a vein in his left arm. Thirst had not been the point of the gesture. Communication had been the point of the gesture.

"Bo," she mouthed again, pointing to herself. Her heart was racing.

Slowly the child curled a stubby index finger toward his own chest. A sound came from the small mouth, hoarse, hard to distinguish. Like the call from a distant hawk.

"I scream because I am a bird." The words of the Paiute chant echoed in Bo's ears. She shook her head.

The boy tried again.

"Ww-eh-po," he whispered, watching Bo avidly.

Somebody had tried to teach him to pronounce his name. Somebody, Bo knew, had labored for months, face close to his, hands on Adam's apples, to teach him there was a sound he could make that identified him. A grin swept her face as she hugged the little boy impulsively. He was warm, soap-smelling, trembly.

"Weppo! Your name's Weppo!"

The boy smiled weakly, his gaze still fastened to her face. And then his eyes closed. The effort had been exhausting.

"This kid's not retarded, he's *deaf!*" Bo yelled. She felt a flush tingle through her cheeks as the earlier dizziness subsided but didn't quite vanish beneath her elation.

Crazy or not, she was right.

"Shh, he needs to rest." Nurse Sailboat pushed Bo toward the door.

"He can't *hear* me; he's *deaf!*" Bo yelled again.

"Well, all the children up here aren't deaf. You'll have to be quiet."

The wary, nervous look on Sailboat was one Bo had seen before.

"Besides, what makes you think he's deaf?"

Bo made a massive effort to control her emotional level.

"My sister was born deaf," she pronounced softly. She never talked about Laurie. *"I know."*

6

Dr. Hound, the Pig

What's going on in here?'' a quiet baritone voice with the barest French accent inquired from the doorway. Andrew LaMarche's gray eyes registered controlled contempt at Bo in the tiny surgical gown. "You must be the worker from CPS."

"Dr. LaMarche," Bo said with a sigh as she tried to pull the gown off and succeeded in stretching the neck of her sweater over her shoulder. Her bra strap had tiny strings fraying from it.

Great. Now on top of everything else he'll think all CPS workers throw bras in the dryer.

"I know you're upset about the Martinelli case; we all are. And I know you hate CPS; we all do. But this kid's *deaf!*"

Andrew LaMarche was taken aback. There was a frenzied logic in whatever the woman was saying. And a certain *feu do joie* that was rather interesting.

"Over coffee?" he suggested. "I was here when the boy was brought in. I'll be supervising his case."

Bo regarded the dapper physician she had hoped to avoid. It was hard to get a sense of the man, who might be modeling for *GQ* or only posing as a doctor to avoid discovery as a retired cold war double agent with unwholesome interests in Argentine coups. Well-cut seal-brown hair, graying at the temples. Equally tidy mustache over courteous smile. Hand-tailored jacket in an exceptional Donegal tweed that would have cost, Bo assessed approvingly, more per yard than she made in a day. If Dr. Andrew LaMarche harbored a secret interest in medieval saddlery or spent his weekends making grape jelly under a rule of silence in some mountain monastery, Bo would not have been surprised. An unusual, courtly man. A gentleman.

"Lean as a hound and shirted in silk," her grandmother would have said.

"Sure," she replied, suppressing a grin at the phrase Bridget O'Reilly invariably used to describe an attractive suitor. "Coffee sounds great." Her grandmother's phrase fit Andrew LaMarche like a kid glove.

The cafeteria at St. Mary's was huge and lit by banks of fluorescent lights concealed above Plexiglas panels. The few off-duty personnel enjoying coffee in small, muted groups had all chosen to face the bank of doors opening onto a cement courtyard. Bo had been there before.

"Do you mind if we sit outside? I could use a cigarette."

Mercifully LaMarche elected to forgo the lecture on lung cancer and merely answered, "Of course."

Bo allowed a spasm of gratitude as she opened Weppo's case file on a cement table.

"What will you do with the boy?" LaMarche asked.

A weak autumn sun was trying to burn off the remaining fog, but a damp chill still hung in the morning air. Bo exhaled the pungent smoke of the French cigarettes she loved and watched it hover in the damp. She wished she knew what she'd do with the boy. She also wished she'd stayed in bed. A deaf child. And a bright one. It would be hard to walk away, like she'd walked away from Laurie.

The memory was painful. She'd been happy to leave her gawky ten-year-old sister behind to go off to college unencumbered by the odious need for sign language. In the little college town of Amherst Bo reveled in the freedom to be normal, to do ordinary things without attracting the attention of strangers. She didn't miss the adoring kid sister with stringy brown hair who wrote strange poetry and signed it with such intensity that perishable objects had to be placed out of reach of her flying hands.

It was Laurie's intensity, Bo realized later in therapy, that was scary. Not Laurie's deafness. The same intensity that Bo fought within herself as if it were one of the *Cwn Annwn*, a hound of hell deep inside her. Years later she would know its name—a neurobiological disorder shared with her sister and called simply manic-depressive illness. But by the time Bo fully understood what she had only sensed in childhood, Laurie was dead.

And now there was another deaf child.

Her sudden attachment to the little boy was inappropriate. Personal. Unprofessional. She was aware of the sense of mission lurking in the air. Delusional. Dangerous.

"I don't know," she answered the doctor's question thoughtfully. "He's deaf. That'll turn up on the tests, won't it? And his name's Weppo or something that sounds like Weppo when you say it without hearing it." Bo ran a hand through her hair. "It's desperately important that he get the right training *now...*"

LaMarche cocked a shaggy eyebrow. "Training? I thought your job was to secure the county's custody of these kids and then stuff them in foster homes until they're beyond hope or else send them back to sadistic killers. Or am I wrong?"

Eat snail trails, Dr. LaMarche.

"You're not wrong. I'm not here to defend the agency I work for. It's a bureaucracy and therefore plagued with bureaucrats. I'm not one of them." Bo felt her green eyes flash and focused pointedly on the limb of a jacaranda drooping over the cement wall of the patio.

"Nobody's happy about what happened to Jennifer Martinelli," she told its fernlike leaves. "But people," she turned to the man across the slab table, "are much less predictable in real life than they are in medical workups. In real life people lie. They conceal things, sometimes even from themselves. And a good act can fool anybody once. That's what happened to Angela Reavey in the Martinelli case. It happens all the time." She exhaled from the side of her mouth with a hiss and stubbed out the cigarette. "But of course you wouldn't know that. You have no contact with people in the real world, only here"—she gestured toward the hospital's five stories—"where you're in control."

LaMarche studied the jacaranda tree as if it were about to speak. Casually he draped both hands around his coffee and assumed the air of someone patiently waiting.

Bo ran a hand through her tousled curls again.

Calm down, Bradley.

"I'd like to talk about this boy, about Weppo," she pronounced deliberately. "I want him to have a chance. I want him to learn ASL before it's too late. This is my case and I may be able to set that up. How old do you think he is, exactly?"

LaMarche shot his cuffs. The woman was unnerving. And unusual. She'd thrown his own anger back in his face with a zest he recognized as practical and intuitive at once. He wondered why she came to work dressed like Paul Bunyan.

"We did a full skeletal X ray," he conceded. "It's hard to say for sure, but from the long-bone maturation I'd guess about four. Why?"

"Four," Bo wrote in the case file and dated the quote. "There's almost no time left."

LaMarche leaned into the conversation, puzzled. "Time for *what?*"

"The imprinting stage for language is birth to five," Bo began, unable to restrain her enthusiasm. "ASL, American Sign Language, is a language, just like English or Spanish or French. And kids learn languages best between birth and five. It goes really sour after puberty too. And Weppo's a boy. Boys are worse for some reason. God knows why. It may have something to do with brain lateralization, which, as you know—"

LaMarche felt his hackles rising. "Wait a minute," he interrupted. "What makes you think you know so much about it? Do you realize you're *diagnosing?*"

Bo's enthusiasm drained away like water through sand. The man was impossible.

"Dr. LaMarche, why do you affect that accent?" she inquired through clenched teeth. "It does detract just a soupçon from your Hitleresque image, you know."

Bo bit her tongue. Irish temper or manic irritability, it wasn't going to help the deaf boy in the hospital bed.

"I'm sorry, doctor." She shifted clumsily to a manipulative simper as LaMarche glanced angrily at his watch.

Doctors!

"I didn't mean to lose it completely. It's just that the little guy needs so much help, and right away, if he's going to have a chance. It would sure speed things up if you'd write a medical recommendation for ASL training . . ." She batted her eyes and stifled a grin. She sounded like Blanche Dubois in *Streetcar*, which wasn't surprising. Her enactment of the role twenty years ago in a college production had been her last occasion to simper.

Unfortunately, Andrew LaMarche's education had included drama.

"It was wise of you to choose social work over acting as a career," he mentioned, stretching tanned fingers in apparent boredom. "Your soothing inanities have failed to impress me. I'm a hopeless elitist *cochon*, I'm afraid. I prefer that diagnoses be performed by *doctors*."

Bo closed the case file with a snap. Who did this posturing, arrogant creep think he was. Descartes?

"*Cochon* means pig, doesn't it, doctor?" She allowed her eyes to widen and pinion his maniacally. Everybody with a history of psychiatric admissions knew how to do "the look." A guaranteed conversation-stopper. "More pompous *boar* than pig. You haven't heard a word I've said. And you never will due to the little-known tragedy of ego-deafness! I'll have the D.A. subpoena you if we need your testimony on Weppo's case. But I doubt that'll be necessary, since you don't want to know anything about him."

LaMarche watched her storm through the glass doors and across the cafeteria. "Pompous boar?" he remarked to his coffee cup. "*Mon Dieu!*" He decided he liked her.

In her car Bo crammed a cassette of Bach's third Brandenburg Concerto into the tape deck. Then she breathed deeply. It helped.

But she was going to have to slow down. Nothing could be worth the risk she was taking. The risk of delusional overinvolvment with a case. A risk that could quickly acquaint her with unemployment, professional and personal ruin. Nothing could be worth that. Not even a deaf boy whose wide eyes reminded her so much of Laurie's.

7

Annie

Bo had forgotten Andrew LaMarche by the time she left the convenience store near St. Mary's at 11:45. A pint of chocolate milk and an unusually fresh cinnamon bagel gave a whole new cast to the day. She'd take a run out to the reservation, interview the woman who found the boy, and then transfer the case. Period. No heroics. No craziness.

The rush of affection she felt for the child, the messianic conviction that she alone had been chosen to save him—these were just typical manic delusions. Delusions so compelling and insistent they could not be ignored. But delusions nonetheless.

Coaxing the rickety BMW east on I-8 toward the mountains that shielded San Diego from the murderous desert heat beyond, Bo pondered the human condition. How much of life's drama would ultimately be understood as the product of brain chemistry? The notion was taboo and probably always would be. The notion that all human behavior, inspired or bestial, had its origins in electrical brain impulses and not in realms of myth. A humbling notion, accepted at last only by those for whom all other options have failed. And a comforting notion, once accepted. Still, Bo reflected, it was odd that this particular case had fallen to her.

The car, overheating in its long climb from San Diego's coastal environs to the higher, drier suburb of El Cajon, relaxed as Bo turned northward off the freeway. El Cajon— "the coffin" in Spanish. Bo shuddered, wishing Estrella hadn't told her what the town's name meant. It was never wise to think about coffins. Bo had seen too many.

First her grandmother's, with the scent of good Irish whiskey wafting over the wake. Then Laurie's, too unthinkable even now. And finally her parents' together, after a faulty wall furnace in a Yucatán resort hotel filled their sleeping lungs with carbon monoxide. Bo's mother had planned the trip for months. She wanted to research Mayan folk music. At the funeral at least twenty-three people had mentioned the unfortunate similarity of their deaths to Laurie's. To curb the disquieting train of thought Bo drew measured breaths of faintly pine-scented air, and exhaled slowly.

Beyond the last suburb of chain-linked subdivisions separated by older mountain homesteads, the road curled gently into another time. From its appearance, Wildcat Canyon Road might still boast actual wildcats, stagecoaches, maybe a Spanish friar harvesting pine nuts in dusty brown robes.

The pignolia pines, clustered in the chaparral between live oaks, cottonwoods, and manzanita, had provided tasty nutmeats to mix with leached acorn meal in Native-American cuisine. Now the tiny morsels went for ten dollars a pound in trendy San Diego culinary boutiques.

At the Barona Reservation Bo discovered a collection of unnumbered dwellings. A cement-block government-issue house here, a trailer there. Winding roads leading off into the dry autumn hills with no clue as to who lived where.

Stopping at a gas station, Bo asked a bronze little girl with a yellow popsicle where Maria and Joe Bigger Fox lived.

"Two houses up. Around the bend on the right," the child answered easily.

Weppo couldn't do that, couldn't name things and their relation to each other. And he never would if somebody didn't teach him.

Bo considered the little girl's black eyes, her lips and clean white teeth forming words. The complexity of it! The unimaginable network of reactions involved in a child understanding a question and framing in a microsecond a picture of the answer. But this child could hear. She'd heard her mother's voice while still in the womb. She'd learned to speak naturally by reproducing human voices around her. And that facility gave her access to reality. But like Laurie, Weppo lacked that facility. Like Laurie, he was locked behind a glass wall watching things that could make no sense because the things had no names. Bo shivered. Nobody should have to live without language. Things were hard enough *with* it.

"You okay, lady?" the little girl inquired.

"Yeah, I'm fine."

Right. I've been sent here by mysterious forces to rescue a child that is not mine from a silence that was my sister's. I'm nuts!

The last of the morning haze burned off as Bo parked in the driveway of Maria and Joe Bigger Fox, who were not inclined to chat.

Maria, tall and rugged in a baggy white T-shirt and jeans, walked with a dancer's gliding movement to her husband's side and remained standing as Bo sank into a cracked Naugahyde recliner. The woman's feet, Bo noted with ill-disguised interest, were clad in lacy high-heeled mules for which Carole Lombard might have traded her eyeteeth.

The ensemble, complemented by a thick braid of graying hair over Maria's shoulder, seemed ingenuous. Even chic. Like the costume of a mature, diamond-hard rock singer.

"Mama came down from that old house at about a quarter to six," Maria Bigger Fox confirmed without emotion. "Said she found a kid up there and had to use the phone. She called 911."

The narrative was neither hostile nor discernibly interested. Merely fact. Bo allowed her own awareness to range over the wide, dark faces, the whole atmosphere of the plain little house, seeking some clue or nuance. Something unsaid or hidden. There was nothing. The husband regarded her from a lopsided green couch in front of a TV, his face as blank as its gray screen.

"Did you notice anything unusual in the neighborhood during the night before Mrs. Garcia found the boy?" Bo asked. The imposition of the term "neighborhood" seemed culturally intrusive. This rugged, silent terrain was a community, but nothing as confining as what "neighborhood" implied. Bo felt a blush of chagrin creeping up her freckled cheeks.

Joe Bigger Fox was as big as a wrestler and looked for all the world like Jay Silverheels doing Tonto, except that his hair was pure white.

"No," he replied with finality. It was clear that he had nothing else to say.

There was, Bo acknowledged ruefully, simply an emptiness in the space between her and the middle-aged Indian couple. As if they were really somewhere else and had replaced themselves with lifelike holograms. The plain living room might be a theatrical set. Bo knew her grasp of the interaction was accurate. She'd seen it before—the Indian way of dissociating from all things white. The misunderstandings. The inevitable power of the dominant culture over the exploited one.

Bo sighed. The Bigger Foxes weren't lying or hiding anything. They just wanted her to leave.

"Well, thanks." She terminated the interview politely. "Could I speak to Mrs. Garcia now?"

Maria glanced through an open window at a trailer behind the house. "She might be asleep. She's an old woman. She sleeps a lot."

"I could come back later," Bo offered.

The Indian woman shook her head. "She won't be here later. She's leaving, on the bus. Going up to Lone Pine for a pow-wow."

"Lone Pine?" Bo was incredulous. She'd been there herself only a few months ago and the coincidence had a prophetic flavor. "Why is she going to Lone Pine?"

"My mother and I are Paiute," Maria Bigger Fox explained patiently, as if speaking to a dense child. "Lone Pine is a town but large sections of it are Paiute Reservation. Independence, Bishop, on up to Mono Lake, and over into Nevada—all Paiute land. Our people are there."

Bo made a feeble attempt at sorting through what information she possessed on California's native people, and discovered a black hole. The Barona had been a local tribe renamed for a Spanish city by Father Junípero Serra or some other coastal padre, but who were the Paiutes?

Her master's thesis at Holyoke had involved a summer of field work among the Iroquois in upstate New York. And she and her ex-husband Mark had spent the first year of their marriage teaching at a Navajo mission school near Los Alamos. None of which gave her a clue about the people in front of her.

"Go on out and talk to her," Joe Bigger Fox rumbled, pointing to the fourteen-foot 1948 Igloo trailer set on crumbling concrete blocks. It had once been silver but now displayed a uniform oxidized powdery gray, pocked with amoebas of rust. A devil's-claw cactus leaned against its side.

"Thank you," Bo repeated, wondering if courtesy demanded a gift of tobacco. It would if these people were Navajo, but they weren't. "Uh, would you like some cigarettes?" She grabbed a fresh pack of Gauloises from her purse.

The Indians looked puzzled.

"French cigarettes?" Joe Bigger Fox accepted. "I guess so."

Bo left the pack on the Formica-topped coffee table and exited, feeling vaguely idiotic.

Why don't you just ask them to autograph your copy of Bury My Heart at Wounded Knee, *you bimbo!*

A couple of mountain jays screeched laconically in a coast live oak towering over half-buried boulders behind the small trailer. The tree's vast lower branches had been propped up with cut logs. Joe Bigger Fox must have done that, Bo decided approvingly. At over sixty feet in height, the tree could be a century and a half old. Annie Garcia's trailer appeared only slightly less venerable.

"What do you want?" a raspy voice not unlike that of the jays called out.

"I'm Bo Bradley, from Child Protective Services," Bo shouted against the trailer's closed door. "I need to talk to you about the little boy you found."

The door was opened by the oldest woman Bo had ever seen. One of Macbeth's witches. An elemental, sculpted in leather. Except this one was wearing track shoes and at least four sweaters over a voluminous corduroy skirt Bo herself might have worn in junior high. Each of the sweaters, Bo noted, bore an identical brown ring at its collar. The trailer's gloomy interior was redolent with the smell of coffee.

"Thank you for talking to me." Bo hunkered on the floor and opened Weppo's case file. There was nowhere to sit except two miniature benches facing a miniature table affixed to the wall. One of the benches was buried under a pile of clothes.

And Annie Garcia would need to sit on the other one. "Can you tell me how long the boy was up in that house?"

The old woman sat on the empty bench. Her eyes showed the telltale milkiness of cataracts.

"Them spirits, they told me something was wrong," she began. "But I went in anyway. I saw the child with blood in its mouth. It might have been a devil, but it wasn't, huh?" Annie cocked her wide brown skull with its high cheekbones toward Bo. "Do you think there's devils?" The words came out in a chuckle.

Bo paused to consider the question, and to buy time. The woman was playing with her, acting crazy to see what she'd do. Beneath the milky glaze the old eyes watched closely. Bo looked straight back and answered truthfully. Nothing less would do.

"There are some weird things, but I don't think there are devils. Mostly, I just don't think we understand much."

"Do you understand about this boy?" The ancient face seemed suddenly wise, as if the woman behind it knew something she wasn't saying.

"You know more about what happened to him than I do," Bo replied. "All I know is that you found him. It's likely that you saved his life. Can you tell me *anything* about how he got here or who was with him or what happened?"

"I told them men," Annie Garcia pronounced, "I never saw that kid at all before I went up there this morning."

Men? What men? The woman must mean the deputy and the paramedic.

"Said they was police," Annie mentioned as if she'd heard Bo's thoughts. "They came after the boy was gone in the ambulance."

Maybe the Sheriff's Department had assigned detectives to investigate, and they'd been up here already? Not a chance. There would be no criminal investigation unless Weppo died or could be shown to be the victim of physical or sexual assault—felony child abuse. Everything else would fall to CPS to investigate. There just wasn't enough man-power in the San Diego County Sheriff's Department to waste detectives on an abandoned child.

"Did these men use that word? 'Police'?"

The Barona Reservation was beyond the jurisdiction of the San Diego Police Department, and squarely within the jurisdiction of the Sheriff's Department. And Sheriff's Department detectives would never identify themselves as police.

"Yeah." Annie Garcia was sure.

"Were they wearing uniforms?" Bo went on. She needed to know who else was investigating the case, if somebody were. In child abuse investigations it wasn't unusual for several sets of people to be out gathering information at once—schools, visiting nurses, an occasional private eye in messy divorce cases, all in addition to law enforcement and CPS.

"Nah."

"Suits and ties?"

"Nah. Just clothes."

Terrific. Two men in clothes.

Bo gave up.

"Have you seen people up at that house before?"

"Yeah. Sometimes."

The woman wasn't being deliberately obtuse. She was Indian, and therefore prone to answer only what she was asked, if that. Indians, Bo knew, were comfortable with allegorical thinking, but put off by the abruptness of whites.

"I'd like to hear," Bo mentioned softly, "about how it was the last time you saw anyone near that place where you found the boy. How was it, then?"

It worked.

"Under the cottonwood, where the trail begins . . . ?" Annie began.

Bo nodded.

"There was a car."

Bo felt her ears lie back, and waited.

There had been a yellow car, Annie Garcia said, the color of a squash. A white man drove it and it had been there yesterday, but not this morning. The car did not, she was almost sure, have California license plates.

A few acorns clattered off the trailer's curved roof as Bo wrote the information in Weppo's case file. It wasn't much.

"If you remember the license number, or the state, or anything else, please call me," she mentioned, and placed her card on the little table. The CPS hotline number was imprinted on it in red.

Annie gazed abstractedly at the painting of daisies in Day-Glo orange on black velvet on the wall. "You care about this child?" she asked.

The question caught Bo off guard.

"Well, yeah. I mean, he's deaf. At the hospital they thought he was retarded. But he's not. In fact, I think he's very bright . . ."

She stood to leave and realized her left leg had fallen asleep. Annie continued to stare at the wall and finally spoke.

"A little child who can't hear," Annie said. "What will happen to him?"

"He'll be in foster homes," Bo explained. "Unless I can find out who he is and where he belongs and then pull a few strings to get him sign language training."

She flexed her left foot and bit her lip at the discomfort. The investigation was going nowhere.

"Do you have children?" Annie asked.

The Indian was getting more information than she was!

"No," Bo answered.

"Why not?"

The old woman remained motionless, a statue in a tableau nobody would ever see. And Bo had not answered that question in ten years. Not since that last bitter discussion with the man who had been her husband, and whom she tried to put out of her thoughts.

Mark David Bradley, both of whose brothers had chosen to be priests, had said simply, "I want to have kids, Bo. We can have our marriage annulled."

"I have a mental disorder," Bo pronounced in the trailer's quiet gloom. "So did my deaf sister. It's called manic-depression. It runs in families. I just couldn't..."—she ran a hand through her hair impatiently—"...run the risk."

Mark hadn't understood. Why did she expect this stranger would? The hell she would not put another person through. The hell that had killed Laurie.

"My sister died when she was twenty," Bo finished the story. "She killed herself."

The ancient figure at the table didn't speak, but Bo felt something envelop her like a shawl. A warmth. An acceptance. She also experienced a near-certainty that she'd see Annie Garcia again. And soon.

8

Like a Dog

Outside the trailer again, Bo blinked in the sunlight and checked her watch. One o'clock. Amazingly, the world had not turned to dust at the words she'd spoken to the old woman. Everything remained intact. It felt good to have said it. Even though it didn't change anything.

Heartened, Bo decided to take a look around before heading back down to San Diego. Take a few pictures to beef up the court report. From her car she grabbed the county-issue Polaroid camera all the investigators carried to photograph injuries. Then she headed for the trail a quarter mile from the Bigger Fox home.

The climb was invigorating. The house was as she'd expected. A shell of a place like others moldering in unexpected mountain niches where some long-ago settler built a dwelling on a trail long since buried in creosote bushes, scrub oak, and deerweed. A gray squirrel scuttled across the tattered roof as Bo entered and prepared the Polaroid camera for flash.

The mattress was there, all right. And the length of white

plastic clothesline that had tied Weppo to it. Bo snapped three pictures of the scene from various angles and squeamishly tugged at the white cord. It came loose easily, but provided no clue as to its origin. Clothesline, Bo admitted, was on a level with aluminum foil, plastic bags, and cheap typewriter paper. Without the packaging, there was no way to identify it.

Something rustled across a boulder outside, and then was silent. She considered briefly how well her Topsiders might stand up to the fangs of a rattler, and smiled. She'd get workmen's comp, anyway.

The mattress was near a stone fireplace that would have been the only source of heat when the house was in use. Idly Bo stirred the ashes with a stick and was surprised to notice the faint orange glow of coals beneath the gray powder. There was a fire here last night.

Suddenly alert, Bo scanned the area more closely. A SpaghettiOs can, raggedly opened with a knife, appeared newer than the other trash littering the floor. Had somebody fed Weppo SpaghettiOs and built a fire before tying him to the mattress and leaving him to die?

She scooped up the ant-infested can and took it outside. She needed to think.

Climbing on a sun-warmed granite boulder, she lay on her back and stared at the sky. A weird day, really.

"So," she yelled at a hawk suspended on a thermal high above, "what's going on? Am I crazy, or is there a pattern to all this?" The hawk broke and swooped lazily toward one of the Laguna Mountains. Bo followed its flight until it vanished. As a bearer of symbolic messages, she decided, this hawk was in the basement.

The warmth of the granite soothed her almost as much as the feel of a paintbrush in her hand. Madge would spit memos, Bo chuckled. County employees were, she was sure, not allowed to lie around on rocks during working hours. If there was no directive to that effect in the procedures manual, Madge Aldenhoven would write one. Fortunately, Madge wasn't here. In fact, nobody was here. And nobody would be likely to be here. So who would leave a deaf four-year-old here, tied up like a dog?

Like a dog.

Bo had heard that phrase before, years ago from the lips of her own pubescent friends.

"Why does your mom keep your sister on a leash? I mean, she looks like a dog!"

Laurie had been wild before their mother gave up trying to teach the toddler to talk, and instead announced that the whole family would learn Sign. Wild, frustrated, angry. In desperation their mother had bought a harness and leash to keep the little girl from running into the street, demolishing grocery store displays or vanishing into parking lots. At eleven, Bo was humiliated. Everybody thought her three-year-old sister was creepy, and so did Bo.

But now she understood why somebody might have to tie down a deaf child who couldn't sign in order to ensure that he'd stay there. Cruel, but perhaps necessary. There would be no way to say "Stay here. I'll be back."

Had whoever it was meant to come back?

Sometimes parents—usually mothers—of abandoned children showed up in a few days, guilty and embarrassed because they'd panicked. Because they'd been unable to cope. Usually they were anxious to get their kids back and just needed a little help. But something about this case felt different to Bo. Desperate parents abandoned children in places where somebody else was likely to pick up the responsibility. Shopping centers, churches, bus stations. And yet the terrain around the crumbling adobe house was devoid of human commerce. Empty. No sense of comings and goings. No sense, in particular, that anyone would ever return. Bo would have bet her last paycheck that whoever left Weppo here was gone, for good. Whoever it was wouldn't be coming back.

The realization made her shiver as she drop-kicked the SpaghettiOs can into the woods and clambered back down the trail. She paused at the dusty Fremont cottonwood where somebody, sometime, had parked a car the color of squash that might or might not have contained a deaf child. A lot of people had parked on the dry shoulder of Wildcat Canyon Road. The ground wore the usual mantle of beer cans, cigarette butts, empty potato chip bags. Bo scuffed the toe of her Topsider through the junk and dislodged a spent shotgun shell. A faded local newspaper, unread. A sandwich bag full of dirt. She turned toward her car parked down the road at the Bigger Foxes'.

But something shimmered at the edge of her field of vision. A scrap of white. Some shred of paper newer, whiter than the others littering the ground. Without knowing why, she retraced her steps and picked it up. A grocery receipt. From someplace called Jamail's. Among the items it enumerated were three cans of SpaghettiOs.

Bo knew of no Jamail's in San Diego, but that meant nothing. The sprawling city had numerous outlying communities. Jamail's could be a convenience store in Lakeside or an independently owned supermarket in Rancho Bernardo. And it probably had nothing to do with Weppo anyway. Still, Bo stuffed the receipt in the pocket of her corduroys and then vowed to go home and get some sleep. The hoped-for flu having failed to materialize, she knew what was coming if she didn't take every precaution. And there was nothing else she could do for Weppo today.

At the reservation gas station pay phone she called Madge Aldenhoven.

"Madge? Bo. I'm just leaving the reservation, and—"

The answering voice bore an uncharacteristic lilt. "Dr. LaMarche phoned me earlier..."

Oh, God. Dr. Kildare and his elephant ego. What's he done? Filed another complaint?

Mentally Bo calculated how long she could live on severance pay and her county retirement refund. About a month and a half.

Madge went on gleefully. "He called to commend you for your handling of the Johnny Doe. He said—"

"He *what?*"

"He said you accurately identified the boy as profoundly deaf and made some helpful suggestions. He also thought you'd want to know the boy's blood and urine workup came back showing he's been on Thorazine. A special attendant will stay with the boy all night while the drug wears off."

Bo eyed the ice machine outside the station and considered buying a bag to put on her head.

Thorazine? The powerful neuroleptic routinely administered in emergency rooms to calm the most disturbed psychiatric patients? Why would anybody give Thorazine to a kid?

"Madge, I'm really feeling rotten..."

And that's not a lie.

"Feverish. Dying, perhaps. There's nothing else I can do on this case today. I need to go home."

Andrew LaMarche's call had saved the day. "That's just fine. You go ahead and take care of yourself," Madge said. "Have you called to arrange foster care yet?"

"No, he's not ready for discharge. I'll do it on Monday, okay?" Bo ended her conversation with the unusually agreeable supervisor and decided to head home.

She chose a Coke instead of the ice and edged onto Highway 67 toward the interstate. In the rear-view mirror she saw a blue Subaru with "Surf 'n' Sun Rent-a-Car" on the plate frames. The car pulled slowly from behind the station.

Of the entire wonderland available to tourists in San Diego County, this particular location would rank last, if it ranked at all. Bo couldn't imagine why the two men in the rented car would possibly be up here in the dusty chaparral on an Indian reservation that did absolutely nothing to encourage visitors.

Thirty-five minutes later, at home in Ocean Beach, she turned right on Narragansett from Sunset Cliffs Boulevard. Her street, she remembered pointlessly, was named for an extinct tribe of East Coast Indians. She wished she would stop remembering things like that. Her mind was weaving garish tapestries. Tying things together, creating meaning where there was none.

In the corner of the rear-view mirror a small blue car containing two men continued on in the boulevard traffic toward Sunset Cliffs and the end of the continent.

"Not possible," she told her gaunt reflection in the mirror. "Don't imagine things!"

But a part of her mind refused to quiet. "Those were the same two men," it insisted. "You're being followed!"

9

The Graveyard Shift

St. Mary's Hospital was quiet as special-duty attendant
Rudy Palachek lowered himself and the blanket-wrapped
child into the defective rocker. Carefully Rudy jammed his
right foot under the mattress of Weppo's bed to compensate.
Without the precaution, the chair would tip over backward
under their combined weight. Rudy made a mental note to
call maintenance first thing in the morning.

The boy, tense at first, relaxed and snuggled against
Rudy's broad chest. Some kids weren't comfortable being
held by a man, but this one seemed used to it. Rudy
wondered if there were a father somewhere who'd ever
rocked his deaf son in the dark. And if so, where was he?

Weppo's breathing slowed to the cadence of deep sleep as
Rudy matched the pace of the rocker to his own heartbeat.
He'd learned that training for the neonatal unit. It always
worked, but Rudy hadn't been sure this time—not with an
active deaf four-year-old coming off Thorazine.

Rudy knew a little about the world of the deaf, learned
from an aunt who'd lived with his family years ago. And

he knew a lot about psychiatric medications, learned from a stint as a psych tech in a Tucson hospital right after he retired from the marines. He knew there could be no conscionable reason for drugging this pale, sturdy little boy who'd quickly learned to catch a Nerf football Rudy had grabbed from the toy room when he came on at 6:00.

Weppo, as Andy LaMarche had explained the boy was to be called, did not lack energy, even after his ordeal in some mountain shack. Rudy tried to remember if there'd ever been a famous deaf quarterback. The way the kid handled the little Nerf ball was something to see. Good manual dexterity. A good eye. And the big grin he'd given Rudy the first time he caught the ball was worth a hundred times the special-duty pay Rudy would get for monitoring vital signs all night.

By 11:30 P.M. all was silent except for the faint buzz of the PA system and occasional hushed voices from the nurses' station. The night shift would be charting, recording the day's vital signs, medications, and reactions on the proper forms. Each shift was supposed to do its own charting, but during the day there was never time. Between rounds and the administering of medications, the night staff would chart all night unless there was an emergency. Rudy flexed his right foot wedged under the mattress and decided to rock his patient until after 12:00 meds when the nurse would come again. If the vital signs remained stable, he'd put the boy back in bed for the night.

Leaning his head against the back of the rocker, Rudy breathed easily and stared at the rectangle of light marking the placement of the door in the wall. Everything was quiet. But he wouldn't fall asleep. He'd never let himself fall asleep even on the easiest night duty. And the discomfort of his foot helped. It was a good start on a quiet night.

Almost.

Something was going on in the hall—an anomalous collection of shadows blurring the outline of the door frame. Somebody standing there. Or two people standing there. But why? There was no family to visit this nameless child.

After twenty-five years as a corpsman and then a civilian medical attendant, Rudy was used to hospital routine, hospital normalcy. A bamboo hut or high-tech teaching hospital in a big city, it was all the same. Staff who had reason to come into a room in the middle of the night did so quickly. The medications, injections, vital signs, turnings, and linen changes all done quickly. Nobody would just stand outside a door.

Probably a late-night confab between relatives of some other kid on the floor, Rudy decided. So why didn't they go up the hall to the visitors' lounge?

Rudy felt a tingling in the large muscles of his legs. A slightly faster heartbeat. He was throwing a little adrenaline in response to the whispering shadows outside Weppo's door. Ridiculous, but the brain will do that, especially at night when it responds to memories of threats long extinct. Rudy knew that, but watched the door closely anyway. The threads of light widened as it opened.

Later Rudy would describe two men standing there, momentarily confused by the darkness and the empty bed. The figures were backlit from the hall, mere silhouettes. One appeared stocky, the other shorter, and thin. They turned toward Rudy and the boy. Rudy remained silent, watching. Whoever they were, they didn't seem to know what the hell they were doing.

"Aw, fuck!" the shorter one drawled, and pushed the

thick one aside. He seemed nervous, in a hurry. Then he pulled something from under his jacket. Something dully silver reflecting the hall light, with a black cylinder attached to it.

In less than a second, thirty years of experience, countless nights in jungle muck trusting nothing beyond his field of vision, registered in Rudy Palachek. With his right foot he pushed hard against the empty hospital bed. It was a gun, he realized just before the chair went over. It was pointed at the sleeping child in his arms!

A muffled pop, like a truck tire blowing out under water.

The chair splintered under his back as it fell. The child began to scream his peculiar scream as running footsteps filled the hall outside.

"Hey! What's going on?"

It was the orderly, running past the door of 323 toward the stairs. His voice, Rudy noticed, was shrill with fear, but it hadn't stopped him from doing his job.

Then another shot.

Children crying. A woman screaming "Oh, my God!" over and over in the hall.

A nurse appeared at the door of 323 and switched on the lights, followed closely by a bewildered security guard. The nurse went pale and then regained her color as Rudy rolled out of the splintered rocker and got to his feet. He still held the screaming child, petting the wiry hair, humming so the boy could feel the sound.

Rudy clenched his teeth over mute rage.

"Call LaMarche," he told the nurse. "And seal this room until the police get here."

A jagged crater disfigured the wall behind him. Rudy looked at it with distaste, and then with renewed fear. In the seven-inch crater was the barest silvery film. Its almost imperceptible sheen caught the light and glistened. Rudy shuddered. The guy had meant business. The sick bastard son of a bitch was a bona fide killer. The silver sheen, Rudy Palachek knew, was mercury.

A hollow-point bullet packed at the tip with a poison so toxic to the human nervous system that a flesh wound could kill. And the deadly package had missed them both by less than two inches.

10

Another Bad Night

Something woke Bo, although she couldn't identify it immediately. An odorous ringing. Her bedroom smelled like colcannon, the buttery combination of potatoes, cabbage, onions, and cream that her grandmother had loved to concoct. The scent washed her in nostalgia. And it kept ringing.

Bo shook her head. Nobody'd cooked colcannon for her in fifteen years. And the ringing was a phone!

She'd gone by the university psychiatric clinic late in the afternoon. Had the initial bloodwork done, got the lithium. It was a safety net, and she'd decided she needed it. Things were getting too haywire, like this potato-scented sound that brought tears to her eyes with its memories. Crazy. She felt the loss of her grandmother as though the feisty old woman had just died. And her parents. And Dr. Bittner. Laurie. AIDS victims. Baby harp seals dead on Canada's frozen coasts. The Black Forest in Germany withering in acid rain. An overwhelming sadness. A bitter, insurmountable loss.

In a psychiatric setting, she mused, somebody would write, "Inappropriate affect, tearful for no reason . . ." on her chart. But there were plenty of reasons, always. And always it was best to block them, keep them from flooding your mind. If you could. The damn lithium, already in her bloodstream, would take three weeks to have any effect.

"It's a quarter of one," she snarled into the bedside phone. "This had better be important."

"Ms. Bradley? This is Andrew LaMarche."

It was going to be bad news. She could tell from the grim tenor of his voice. The scent of grieving in the room. The howling of a mythological crone her people nicknamed Cally over the sea outside.

"What's happened?" Had Weppo died? The light in those bright eyes gone flat? Bo gripped an edge of the plaid sheet and noticed that her knuckles were white.

"Somebody tried to kill the boy," LaMarche pronounced unevenly. "Somebody came in this hospital, two men, armed, for the sole purpose of killing a child. And they shot an orderly. His name was Brad Sutin. He was only twenty-one. He's dead."

Two men? Maybe you weren't imagining it after all.

"But Weppo . . . ?" Bo fought a deep need to scream.

"There was a special-duty attendant, a man I knew in the service named Palachek. He saw it coming and hit the floor. He was holding your boy. He saved the child's life."

The nightmare. Not to be understood. But Weppo was alive, not like Laurie so finally still in velvet and Irish lace.

"I'll be there in twenty minutes," Bo replied. A taste of salt alerted her to the fact that she'd bitten her lip.

"A semi-jacket hollow point .38 packed with *le mercur—*"

the doctor was raging in a bilingual frenzy. Bo wondered where he was from.

"I'll be there as soon as I can," she repeated, and hung up.

She had to go, for a multitude of reasons.

Weppo was, legally, in nobody's hands at the moment. Nobody had legal jurisdiction yet over a child who'd come close to death twice in the last twenty-four hours.

Twice!

"And the third's the charm." She rolled her Rs bleakly. The racial memory of a thousand Celtic ancestors thrummed in her skull. That was the reason Celtic designs were often in *fours*—to trick fate. Weppo would not survive a third brush with death.

And the legal tangle would take all night.

St. Mary's would have procured a permission-to-treat from a judge when the boy was brought in. In the absence of a parent or legal guardian, it was the only way they could legally provide care for the child. But St. Mary's had no responsibility to protect Weppo from assassins. In fact, the hospital's real responsibility lay in protecting the hundreds of other children under its roof from the danger now represented by a deaf four-year-old. A four-year-old somebody was trying to murder. If his medical condition were stable, St. Mary's would have to discharge Weppo immediately. But discharge to whom?

It was a weekend. Legal limbo. No court in session. The paperwork that would assure San Diego County's custody of Weppo wouldn't be filed until Monday, under normal circumstances.

Normal?

Bo allowed herself to laugh hysterically while pulling clean clothes from a laundry basket. Lois Bittner had pointed out several hundred times, "When you're feeling crazy, is best to look sane." Good advice.

Bo put together her sanest outfit—a luxuriantly draped wool skirt and leather boots that, with a silk blouse and blazer, made her look like a spinster professor of English literature at some preppy East Coast university. Very sane. She looked around for the matching briefcase and found it, unaccountably, in the bathroom closet behind a stack of furnace filters. Bo wasn't sure her wall furnace had a filter, but they'd been on sale. She tried to confine her typically manic spending sprees to practical items. The filters managed to convey a spirit of practicality, lying there in the closet. A focus. Bo felt better.

She'd have to call a district attorney from the hospital, and then go to the office and complete the eight different forms necessary to secure the court's and the Department of Social Services' custody of Weppo. The D.A. would have to sign them, grant the petition. Only then could plans be made for Weppo's next move.

Bo picked up the phone.

"Madge!" she yelled into Aldenhoven's answering machine at home. "I know you're asleep, but wake up! It's an emergency! Somebody's tried to shoot my NPG at St. Mary's, and killed an orderly. We need a petition *now*, and how do I find a foster home that can protect him? Somebody's trying to *kill* him, and St. Mary's is going to want to discharge him first thing in the morning. I'm on my way there now. Get up!"

Mildred hadn't stirred from her bedside basket as Bo opened the door to a hazy fog less dense than the night before. Something was taped to the outside knob. A flier, Bo assumed. A new pizza parlor. A car wash. She pulled the white sheet loose and glanced at it absently.

It was a picture, cut from a magazine. A picture of a fox

terrier. The dog's head had been ripped off. The words "STAY THE FUCK AWAY" were block-printed in pencil across the bottom.

Oh, shit!

Running back inside she grabbed Mildred still wrapped in her blanket, and stuffed dog-and-blanket inside her jacket. So much for looking sane.

"No way!" she promised the dog. "This is crazy!"

11

"Grandmother, Persevere..."
— *Kiowa Song*

Annie Garcia sat halfway down the bus's left side, against the wall. It had been difficult, changing buses in Los Angeles, but a Mexican had helped her with her plastic bags full of clothes. She'd given him one of the tuna sandwiches Maria packed for the trip. Annie didn't like tuna anyway.

Outside the tinted windows darkness roiled and flowed across the desert floor. Nothing to see, and she'd seen it before. To see the desert, Annie had been taught well as a child, you have to touch it. With your feet and hands and eyes. The desert will not sing its stories for a passing glance.

Maria had not wanted Annie to take the bags of clothes.

"Why do you want to haul all that stuff up to Lone Pine?" Joe had asked as he heaved the bags into the truck for the trip to the little bus station in El Cajon. "You'll just have to haul it back."

But Joe was Barona, not Paiute.

Maria merely saw, and said nothing. "Behind the blanket'' it was called. The Paiute way of not being there in your mind.

Annie shifted her weight on the scratchy seat and tried again to sleep. Ten hours on a bus was agony. She was glad it was the last time.

Lodging her tongue in the gap left by a broken tooth thirty years ago, she hummed softly. The sound in her head helped her drift off. Not really asleep, but not awake. She heard the cry-dance singers, and saw a star. A dark star against a white background. Just a small, plain star with figures on both sides—numbers. She could see a 3, and a 5, and a 1. There were others, but they were too hazy. The star was smaller than the numbers, and above them. It wasn't much of a star.

The bus stopped briefly in Mojave and its lurch made the image shatter like bits of a mirror. But she remembered. A star and 3, 5, 1. A spirit-message. Annie sighed. Why did the spirits choose for their endless gifts old people who only wanted to rest? Why not the young, who'd be awake and paying attention? And what did it mean, this star?

The bus rounded a corner and narrowly missed a car parked on the street. Annie watched the maneuver, detached. But then it came to her. The license plate! The plate on the parked car reminded her of that other car. The one the white woman wanted to know about. The white woman who said she was loco, and worked to take care of hurt little children. How loco could that be? The spirits must like the white woman, and the child who couldn't hear. The star and the numbers were on the yellow car!

In the darkened bus Annie forced herself to remember until the rest stop at Inyokern. The card the woman had given her was in her purse.

With wrenching effort she crept from the bus when it

stopped in the shadowy little desert town and found a phone.

"Child Abuse Hotline," a young male voice answered. "Yes, we'll accept charges."

"I call Barbara Bradley," Annie read the name off the card, "about the little boy who can't hear."

"You have a message for Bo Bradley?"

"Yes."

"Well, tell me and I'll get the message to her. Who may I say it's from?"

Whites and their rude, abrupt ways. Who knew who it was from? It was from the spirits.

"The license plate on the yellow car..." Annie tried again.

"Wait a minute. Who is this?"

"I found the child." Annie identified herself proudly. "I saved his life! And tell her a 3 and a 5 and a 1 and a star. I'm going to Lone Pine now, going to a pow-wow."

"I need to know who—"

Gently Annie replaced the receiver. The white woman would be happy to get the spirit message. And Annie would be happy to get a cup of vending machine coffee.

The hotline worker doodled threes and fives and ones on a notepad and considered whether or not to convey the message to Bradley over in the court unit. The call was obviously a joke. Or some crazy on Bradley's caseload. Probably a schizophrenic. He'd read somewhere that they talked in numbers.

Then he remembered that Bo Bradley worked in Madge Aldenhoven's unit. "Monster Madge," who'd get you fired for not completing a DSS315 phone memo form as the procedures manual required.

The hotline worker had just bought a new car. With stiff

payments. Quickly he filled out the DSS315 and dropped it in the out basket. Then, to be doubly efficient, he phoned Bradley's office. She wouldn't be in at 2:00 in the morning, but he could log the call and cover his tail.

"Bueno," Estrella Benedict answered yawning, forgetting where she was. "I mean Child Protective Services, Bo Bradley's desk."

"What are you doing in the office at this hour?" The hotline worker was amazed.

"An emergency. What in hell do you think we're doing? Folk dancing? What's up?"

"Got a message for Bradley. Just came in long-distance. A crazy, I think. An old woman. Said she was going to a pow-wow in Lone Pine. Something about a yellow car. And a star. She said, '3, 5, 1, and a star.'"

The worker could hear a small dog yipping in the background. Why would there be a dog in the office? It must be true what everybody said about the court investigators. Too much stress.

"Wow," Estrella breathed. "That's the Indian! I'll get the message to Bo over at the hospital. Thanks!"

The hotline worker hung up, shaking his head. Barking dogs at the office at 2:00 A.M.? Indians with stars? Maybe he'd go back to school. Maybe computers.

12

My God, that's great!'' Bo exclaimed into the third floor nurses' station phone as Estrella relayed Annie Garcia's message. "Let me get it down..." She gestured to Police Detective Bill Denny, who was standing with LaMarche and Madge Aldenhoven. "A 3, a 5, a 1, and a star, right?"

Andrew LaMarche, having examined Weppo and arranged for an army of private security guards who would patrol the hospital until further notice, could not bring himself to leave. The shooting reminded him of a past in which people were blown to bits for obscure reasons in Asian jungles. He'd joined the Marines after his freshman year at Tulane. Now he tried to remember why. Something to do with adventure, with a need for discipline, with a young man's hunger for a concept of honor. He'd wanted to learn about honor. And he had. Its antithesis could be found in the armed invasion of a sanctuary for children. The fact made him deeply angry, and deeply concerned for the deaf little boy somebody was determined to kill.

As Madge Aldenhoven orchestrated by phone the legal

intricacies of the boy's status, he listened and somberly made medical recommendations the Department of Social Services would be obliged to follow. Among these was a strong suggestion that Weppo's foster care arrangements include extensive training in American Sign Language. Aldenhoven, efficient even at 2:00 A.M., made a note of the recommendation. It would be included in the court orders now hurriedly being prepared.

Bo watched the two of them from the nurses' station. LaMarche rumpled and steely-eyed. Madge was out of character in mindlessly donned sweatshirt and immense khakis that must belong to her husband. As she talked on the phone Madge held up the pants with her free hand. To keep from laughing Bo thought about Annie Garcia.

How had the old Indian woman done it, she wondered. How had she called up a visual memory that could have had no meaning for her when it was encoded? No reason to remember.

Tucking the receiver under her chin, Bo handed the slip of paper to Denny. "This may be part of a license number from a car seen near where the boy was found," she told him.

"I'll see if we've got anything," Denny responded, and headed for a wall phone.

"Bo, are you . . . okay?" Estrella whispered in the empty office, as if somebody might overhear, guess the secret. "I mean, this is enough to make *anybody* crazy, having a kid on your caseload shot at!"

Bo cupped a hand over the phone's mouthpiece. "No, I'm not okay. Not since early this morning. But I've got the lithium already. I'm on top of it."

She knew she was talking too fast, showing too much feeling. Estrella didn't miss it.

"Oh, *sheet!*" she shouted. "Bo, you've got to get away

from this. Get away from Madge before she figures out there's something wrong with you. She'll crucify you."

"I know," Bo agreed. "But, Es, I just have this feeling. If you could see him, see Weppo . . . he's so . . . *alone*."

"He's not alone! He's got the three biggest bureaucracies in San Diego on his side. Cops, social workers, doctors. He'll be fine. But you won't . . ."

Bo could see the boy, awake in his room across from the nurses' station. An armed uniformed cop stood at the door. Rudy Palachek was inside, teaching the child to sign colors. They'd mastered red. Weppo was still alive and had learned to sign a color. Bo couldn't find words to explain the miracle.

"Es," she whispered, "I can't walk away from this. I'll be all right. Don't worry."

"I *will* worry. Get home as soon as you can. Or come over to our place. I'll have Henry make up the guest bed. And don't worry about Mildred. She's right here, and she's going home with me. Nobody's going to hurt her. Henry'll see to that. You know how he loves her."

"Thanks, Es," Bo whispered. After hearing of the threat, Madge had arranged for Estrella to pick up the dog from the hospital before going over to the office to help draft the voluminous paperwork required by the situation. A district attorney was on his way to sign the petition. Bo experienced an exaggerated wave of affection for her coworkers that brought tears to her eyes.

A small voice warned, "Delusional. Don't get smarmy!" But Bo didn't have time to listen. Bill Denny was waving the scrap of paper bearing a star and three numbers.

"Gotta go, Es." Bo hung up the phone.

Madge and LaMarche appeared to be arguing as Bill Denny passed them. Bo heard her name in the conversation.

"Bingo!" Denny smiled grimly. "A stolen car. Registered

in Houston to a guy named Barry Velk. He reported it stolen two weeks ago to the Houston P.D. The star was the big clue. Texas plates, the older ones, have a star over the numbers. This one was 351-687. Squash yellow, just like you said. A Mercury. And . . .''

Bo was elated. "And this Velk? Who is he? Does he know anything about Weppo?''

Bill Denny shook his head. "Nah. When the auto theft guys called him yesterday to tell him his car was found here he just said he went to a movie one night, and when he came out, his car was gone. But—''

"The car was found yesterday in San Diego? Where?''

Bill Denny pushed the loose frame of his aviator glasses up an aquiline nose and sighed. "Downtown. Early morning. Some wino was gonna sleep in it. But if you'd slow down and let me finish, I'd tell you the big news.''

Bo bit her lower lip and was silent.

"The wino found a stiff in the car. White male. Young. Maybe twenty-three. OD'd on some bad stuff he'd just bought on the street. The needle was still in his right hand. Lotta tracks. The guy was a heavy user. Medical examiner'll do an autopsy on Monday.''

Death. Everywhere. Bo could see the nightmare settling in a nest made of the bones of poets. Could see a painting of the scene she might do herself. The feverish, spavined mare. Screaming. Nesting on a mound of bones.

"Watch out, Gormfhlaith,'' her grandmother's voice cautioned in Gaelic. In the ancient tongue her name meant "strange woman.'' It was appropriate, she acknowledged. Totally.

"Are you okay?'' Bill Denny inquired.

Under the detective's red nylon windbreaker Bo noted the bulge of a gun. And a rumpled T-shirt. Bill Denny had been pulled out of bed like the rest of them. She wished she could be as calm.

"There wasn't anything to identify the . . . the corpse, in the car?"

Denny yawned. "Nothing. Clean as a bone in the desert. And besides, there may be no connection between the stiff and the kid. We've got some Indians downtown, street types, druggies. Maybe one of them borrowed a car from our guy in Houston and drove home to see Mom. Maybe the guy was up on the reservation making a drug drop. There's still nothing to connect him to the kid."

Bo knew Denny was right. Annie's message hadn't brought them any closer to solving anything. She felt like throwing up.

And then she remembered something—the grocery receipt.

"Is there a grocery in Houston called Jamail's?" she asked the detective.

His eyelids were at half mast.

"How should *I* know? I've never been in Houston. Why?"

"I found a receipt," Bo raced through an explanation, "up at the reservation. And SpaghettiOs. They were *on* the receipt."

"Spaghetti on a receipt . . . ?" Bill Denny was beginning to look wary. Bo wanted to strangle him. *Why* were they all so slow?

"If I give you the receipt, will the police check it out?" She tried to slow down.

"Sure. No problem."

"When?"

"Monday, probably. This case will have to go through the assignment desk. I'm backed up for weeks. The department'll assign another detective. It'll take a while."

Monday! He'll be dead by Monday!

Across the hall the pale child with wild, wiry hair touched a red plastic truck, a red notebook, the red print on a hospital menu, and then signed "red."

"Excuse me." Bo smiled at the detective, and went to Weppo's door.

It was going to be up to her. She'd known it somehow all along. The message in the fog. Caillech Bera wailing . . . to her. The rest of them didn't understand, were too slow, simply couldn't see. She would have to solve the mystery of Weppo's identity quickly, if he were to survive. And she would have to do it alone.

"Kid's crazy about colors," Palachek mentioned. "I just thought I'd entertain him for a while until the excitement dies down, see if he could pick up a little signing. He loves it. But all he wants to know are colors."

"Where did you learn to sign?" Bo asked the beefy ex-marine.

"My aunt was deaf," he explained. "From Rocky Mountain spotted fever. She lived with us. We all learned to talk on our hands."

Incredible.

"Bo?"

It was Madge, her eyes following Bo narrowly.

"I've decided to take you off this case. We'll let the higher-ups handle it. It's too dangerous, after the threat on your door . . . and you, well, I just think it's best."

How much do you know, Madge? How much do you suspect?

The supervisor's gaze was critical, judgmental.

"Dr. LaMarche does not agree."

"Absolutely not!" Andrew LaMarche seethed. His tie was askew and his chin revealed a salt-and pepper stubble. "Ms. Bradley actually *cares* about this child, unlike some of your other . . ."

Madge stiffened as Bo shot the doctor a look of gratitude. What she saw in the man's face was surprising. Fondness. Concern. A disarming genuineness. Andrew LaMarche, she realized with bemused amazement, actually liked her. Or was she imagining that too?

The intense state she was sliding into could produce a knock-your-socks-off romantic interest out of thin air. Was it only three years ago, Bo tried to remember, that she'd responded avidly to a similar look on the face of a marine biologist ten years her junior, only to tire of the affair with equal abruptness three weeks later? The manic's pattern of hypersexuality. To be avoided at all costs.

Andrew LaMarche, she decided firmly, was just a workaholic pediatrician with a messy situation on his hands. A messy situation dumped by fate into the lap of the one person with sufficient vision to comprehend its urgency. The one person mysteriously destined to protect this deaf little boy. Still, she wished she could tell the overwrought doctor about what she was going to do to help the boy. Something in his changeable gray eyes, now slate-colored from exhaustion, would see the sense behind the madness. Bo trusted her judgment on that, and was grateful for the fact of it. Andrew LaMarche was on her side.

"There is nothing but reality," she mumbled to herself.

"What?" LaMarche asked.

"I said, I have to make a phone call."

In minutes a long-distance directory assistance operator confirmed Bo's grasp of the information provided by Bill Denny. There *was* a grocery in Houston called Jamail's. Three more calls and Bo had reservations on an oddball flight to the Texas city leaving in less than two hours. A San Francisco-to-Houston-via-San-Diego carrier downed in San Diego when its landing gear refused to retract. They were fixing it, even though the San Diego airport was closed, technically, until 6:00 A.M. Too good to be true. A weekend, she could fly to Houston and back without anyone knowing where she had gone.

"Don't worry." She waved to Andrew LaMarche.

"You too, Madge."

They looked like puppets as she left, marionettes dangling on invisible strings in a hospital corridor. Already a great distance from her.

"There is *nothing* . . ." Lois Bittner's warning began, but Bo snuffed it.

Yeah, but this is my *reality. Who's to say it isn't the real one?*

There was no answer.

13

The Bayou

Deely Brasseur stirred some "dirty rice" over a butane stove and broke an egg into the steaming bean-and-rice mixture. The sun came up slow in the swamp. Easy. Like the breathing of someone asleep. No light touched the raggedy, nasty curtains yet, and Deely cooked by the light of a candle. Just one candle, so as not to draw attention. But the sun's light would steal on. One more night was gone.

The Atchafalaya Swamp had its secrets, and Deely was one of them, hidden among its cypress stumps and Spanish moss like a snake. Her nephew Raveneau's place, over the state line from Texas into Louisiana. Just a fishing shack. But safe as a prayer. They wouldn't find her there.

Deely smoothed the cotton skirt over her ample belly and bowed her head.

"Thanks to the Lord," she intoned, "for this here food. Watch over my baby, wherever he be."

The child might as well be hers, even with his pale white skin. She alone had cared for the poor, sickly thing after the mama was called. Cared for the mama too. Right up to the child's birth when Julie Lynn Rowe, at seventeen, hemorrhaged to death in her own attic. Miz Rowe had said there couldn't be no doctor. And the baby had cried and cried.

"Wilhelm," Julie whispered. "His name is Wilhelm, for our grandfather." And then she was dead. That was four years ago.

Deely ate in silence.

Some folks was given one thing to deal with in life, and some folks another. She'd done her best to deal with what she was given—a secret locked in an attic. But when she saw the bags of quicklime hid in the garage, she knew her best wouldn't be good enough. Not anymore.

She'd made a phone call when she saw what was going to happen. It would defy *God*, what was going to happen!

And it worked, as she hoped it would. Julie's brother, Kep, all wide-eyed and stumbling from the drugs, came and took the child away.

Deely had done what could be done.

Now she feared for her life, and hid, and waited for it to be over. Outside, the first light gleamed dully on swampwater gray as gunmetal. Deely opened her Bible to the part about Moses. About how when the mama couldn't hide her baby no more from Pharaoh, she put him in a little handmade boat down among the bullrushes, and hoped someone would feel pity. And someone did. Moses' mama's plan worked. Deely prayed hers would too.

Marguerite would send word soon, from Houston.

It wouldn't be much longer.

14

Houston Heat

The airport was swollen with the spoor of mildew as Bo
disembarked from the plane at 9:30. The odor hit her like an
oozy wind, like the air from a bag of damp, forgotten
swimsuits. Decay, mold, fungus. This city, she determined,
must be like a huge toadstool spawned in the brackish
sludge of below-sea-level wetlands. The realization made
her think of the gills she and every other mammal had
possessed before birth. Houston's air made her wish she still
had them.

A fitful nap on the plane had been troubled by an
increasing unease, paranoia, and knifelike sensory perceptions the lithium wouldn't diminish soon enough. At one
point she'd wakened to the sharp scent of rotting peaches,
although of course there were no rotting peaches immediately noticeable on the plane. There would be, sixteen rows
away, a child with a lollipop or a woman wearing some
fruity perfume. The man in the aisle seat to Bo's left had
meticulously folded his *Los Angeles Times* so that only half
a column headline was visible.

Detroit Mar
Drops Not

The meaningless words leaped at her repeatedly like flickering strobe lights. She couldn't ignore them.

Over El Paso a woman in the seat in front of Bo had adjusted her seat-back so many times Bo could only conclude that the woman actually wanted to be strangled by an irate fellow passenger before touching ground. The in-flight magazine provided distraction; Bo memorized its editorial roster to focus her attention, and wondered idly why they'd chosen a printer in Chibougamau, Quebec.

She was delighted when the plane finally taxied to its gate at Houston's Intercontinental Airport, and she could move. Moving, walking, provided sensory experience that was real. Diminished that weird playground shrinks loved to call "internal stimuli"—the fascinating, then gradually terrifying panorama of intense perceptions created in a brain no longer able to filter, arrange, and categorize the million messages coming at it. A brain that would seize any stimulus—an odor, a color, a snatch of conversation—and amplify it randomly.

It was good to walk, but the heat was astonishing. Especially in a wool skirt and boots.

Must you always look like the publicity agent for a foreign circus, you jerk?

It hadn't occurred to her that Houston might be warmer than San Diego. Among the litany of other things that hadn't occurred to her, it seemed a mere oversight. Nothing compared to the oversight that had brought her here. The one in which she'd forgotten that this particular grandiose delusion would without doubt cost her her job while racking up astronomical credit card charges. Which would have to be paid. And with what? Bo glanced at her image in a vending machine mirror and wondered if, after twenty years of struggle, the idiosyncratic wiring in her brain were going to win after all. The specter of herself as a lunatic bag lady lurked relentlessly just below consciousness. A doppelgänger, a dark and ruined twin.

Nothing lay between her and that ever-present ghost but hard-won insight.

You're delusional, Bradley. But you're here. Eat something, pop your lithium, and see what you can find out. Then get back to San Diego and pretend this never happened.

Over rubbery and unnecessarily yellow scrambled eggs in an airport coffee shop, Bo looked around. A lot of Stetson hats and cowboy boots. A chantlike drawl in conversations. A propensity for repetition in verb phrases.

"Ah *told* him, ah said, 'Jack,' ah said . . ."

Bo could, after three minutes, replicate the Texans' drawl precisely. Just another perk from a mental disorder that would guarantee many of its victims employment as actors. There was always an up side. She clung to the thought as she negotiated the rental of the cheapest car possible.

Houston's phone directory gave a Shepherd Drive address for the grocery called Jamail's. Bo bit the end off a ballpoint pen while plotting her course on a map provided by the rental car service. The airport was out in the middle of nowhere, miles from the city.

On the long, humid drive she noticed a plethora of billboards promoting the candidacy of a woman named Rowe for a seat on the state senate.

"Reclaim the future; VOTE ROWE!" the signs urged. The candidate looked competent enough. Sleek. Shrewd. Mature and tough, yet costumed in a soft blouse accented with a floppy bow that managed to suggest warmth, humor. But the eyes . . . Even with professional makeup and a heavily filtered camera lens, there was no disguising the emptiness of those wide-set eyes. A chameleon's eyes that would reflect whatever you wanted to see. A manipulator's eyes, cool as caves.

Bo only saw one billboard for Bea Yannick, Rowe's opponent. She looked for all the world like an ex-nun who could, if necessary, kick ass.

"I'd vote for Yannick in a second," Bo mentioned to the dashboard, and clicked on the radio. An incredibly long version of "Mamas, Don't Let Your Babies Grow Up to Be Cowboys" lasted to the Westheimer exit off the 610 loop.

From the long road behind her the skyline of Houston had looked like a gleaming miniature landscape of chrome Legos and milk cartons painted black. The city's splendid architecture was dwarfed to toy size by endless sky. In fact, the cluster of steel-and-glass buildings appeared to be sinking even as it struggled upward. The sky was pushing it down.

It occurred to Bo that Texas songs were always about the sky because there simply wasn't anything else. No hill, no mound, not even a ripple of earth to break the dizzying sweep of the eye toward infinity. "Flat," she decided, was a term insufficient to the terrain. It was more than that. It was actually a negative pull, an inverted gasp of ground beneath a firmament so boundless it might threaten the sanity of even those who weren't already pushing the edge.

To her right, below the 610 loop, a broad tube of greenbrier and blackberry vines woven over loblolly pines, black hickory, and oak trees snaked under the overpass. Nearly strangled by poison ivy, a small sign identified the winding jungle as Buffalo Bayou. Impossible not to wonder what buffalo might do in a bayou. She exited the freeway on Westheimer; a street named Buffalo Speedway answered the question. They would speed.

Bo shook her head. This wouldn't do. Fortunately, the grocery was less than a mile away.

The store's parking lot teemed with Mercedeses and other cars too pricily obscure for Bo to name. Boys in white dress shirts carried even the smallest packages for the grocery's well-dressed patrons. No one seemed to notice the heat.

Money, Bo concluded. Megamoney. Jamail's was not in a slum. Taking the grimy receipt from her purse, she went inside.

"That?" a gum-chewing cashier answered. "Sure, it's ours. Whaddaya think? It's the Rowes' account too." She pointed to a code at the top. "M-A-C-R-O. That's MacLaren Rowe. The Rowes. You know."

Bo didn't know.

"Tia Rowe?" The girl was growing impatient. "Her name's all over town!"

"You mean the one that's running for—?"

"Yeah. That's her."

"Uh, do the Rowes live near here?" Bo pressed.

"Yeah . . . over in River Oaks. Why do you wanna know?"

Cover your tracks, Bradley.

"They've contributed *so* much to owah food drive for the homeless," Bo drawled sweetly. "Of co-wus they wanted to remain a*non*ymous, but Ah'm afraid this receipt gave them away. Such *de-ah* people!"

Bingo!

The Rowe mansion was Georgian Colonial, its brick facade buffered by leatherleaf mahonia shrubs and two geometrically placed magnolia trees. Bo would not have been surprised to see Scarlett and Rhett lusting in one of the upstairs windows tucked under overhanging eaves. She was surprised though to see an aluminum attic vent set in the shake shingles. It spoiled the house's lines.

Climbing the broad brick steps beneath white pillars supporting a Georgian pediment, Bo was unnerved a second time by the door. Its color had been identified in her childhood crayon box as Indian Red. To her artist's eye, the color was an assault. The door's brass knocker had been crafted to resemble a cluster of grapes. Bo grabbed it anyway, and knocked.

"Yes?" A uniformed maid inquired.

"May I speak to Tia Rowe?" Bo didn't really expect to speak to the much-publicized candidate.

The entry hall bore the unmistakable imprint of a decorator who had fought and lost the battle to meld the house's architecture to someone's, probably Tia Rowe's, demand for a "Country French" look. A reproduction Louis XIV tapestry screen in which Breton peasants sculled through a maze of vines stood beside a cherry table whose cabriole legs seemed bent under the weight of an oversized brass spittoon full of chrysanthemums. Bo shuddered.

Tia Rowe, with her flat billboard eyes, also possessed the artistic sensibilities of a *nouveau riche* pack rat. Bo cast about for something to say, some way to gain entry.

On a wall beneath the first landing of an elegant staircase, a jarring collection of framed antique photographs failed to create warmth and appeared merely shabby against bright wallpaper featuring more tortuous vines, lavender blossoms, and sunflowers. One of the photographs seemed familiar.

"Miz Rowe don't allow no reporters at the house," the maid insisted, and began to close the door.

"Wait!" Bo exhaled.

The sepia-toned studio portrait of a boy in knickers and a belted jacket was more than familiar—it was Weppo! It didn't just look like the wiry-haired child in the hospital bed, it *was* that child. The same unmistakable hair, the same wide eyes and pale, thin lips. The boy in the picture was a few years older than Weppo, maybe six or seven. But it was *Weppo* at six or seven. And at the turn of the century!

"I'm not a reporter," Bo explained. "I'm here because

of the boy, because of Weppo," she gestured toward the picture. "Please!"

Bo saw the reaction, the involuntary pull of scalp muscles behind the ears. The moment of recognition. And then panic. The maid knew exactly what Bo was talking about, and was terrified.

"Go on outta here," she whispered. "Go 'way! It ain't safe."

Jamming a toe of her boot against the door, Bo slipped one of her business cards with her home number written on it into the young black woman's hand.

"Somebody tried to murder him," Bo hissed through clenched teeth. "Call me."

The door closed in her face.

15

Chivas, Neat

Only two people were present in Houston's Oak Arbor Country Club bar when it opened at 11:00. One of them was the bartender.

"The usual, Mr. Rowe?" he inquired as if there were the remotest possibility that Mac Rowe would start his day with anything other than scotch, neat, with a water back. It was common knowledge that Mac never drank the water. It was also common knowledge that this would not be the aging playboy's first drink of the day.

MacLaren Rowe rested his elbows on the massive bar salvaged from a long-vanished resort hotel in Galveston, and nodded absently. He felt like one giant chicken dropping. The sharp pain in his stomach was getting worse. And he looked as bad as he felt.

With Deely gone, he couldn't find anything. The cuffs of a stained shirt flapped without cuff links over trembling fingers. He had to hold the glass with both hands.

"Election's in three days," the bartender noted conversationally. "Looks like the missus'll be our next state senator, huh?"

Everybody on staff at the heavily paneled Oak Arbor Club continued to refer to Tia Rowe as Mac's "missus." A polite tribute to four generations of Rowe membership in a club so rooted in Southern tradition it would still accept Confederate money. The truth was, Mac had known for two decades, if Tia Rowe were married to anything, it was to the Rowe shipping fortune, accumulated when slaves still loaded bales of raw cotton onto vessels bound for Europe from Galveston. And the Rowe fortune was gone, drained into Tia's wardrobe, Tia's decorators, Tia's thousand charitable and cultural endeavors that were never substantial enough to be acknowledged beyond the society pages.

Mac Rowe hadn't regarded Tia as his wife in longer than he could remember. The thought gagged him, like the idea of bedding a bag of broken glass.

"We'll see." He smiled crookedly. "How about another scotch?"

Tia might win, he acknowledged to himself. She wanted it badly enough and whatever Tia wanted, Tia got. He'd signed over a power of attorney to her the last time he wound up detoxing at that pansy-ass health spa in San Antonio. Before he got out, Tia'd sold the last of the Rowe property—three square blocks of hand-fired brick warehouse, right on the Galveston Strand—to a mall developer. The money had financed her campaign and an endless parade of consultants, promoters, handlers. A win would present Tia Rowe with ample opportunity for replenishing the coffers and supporting herself in the style to which he had accustomed her.

But first she had to win the election. And it was close. Last week's poll had shown Bea Yannick running only six percent behind. A Yankee yokel with nothing but a grass-roots organization, Yannick had come out of nowhere and put the fear of God into Tia Rowe.

Secretly Mac was glad Yannick had dragged his wife into deep water. With any luck, she might drown. Mac often wished he'd killed her himself, years ago. She'd brought him down, just like his mama said when he announced his marriage to the flamboyant Northerner. Mac pondered how much further down he could go before the end, and realized he didn't care.

Deely had left, suddenly. And the imbecile child his daughter had produced was gone too. Mac didn't care about the kid, but Deely had cleaned up after Mac, kept his clothes clean, made sure he had a meal now and then. The new maid didn't know her ass from a soup can and jumped out of her skin at the fall of a shadow.

Mac ordered another scotch, just to kill the pain in his gut. He wondered how Tia was going to bankroll the final days of the campaign. There was nothing left, but Tia kept buying more TV slots, spending like she owned a bank.

And maybe she did.

There was, he admitted, one helluva lot Mac Rowe didn't know about his wife.

16

Return Flight

The rental car had developed an annoying squeak somewhere near the left rear wheel. It made Bo think of toys. Old, forgotten toys with squeaking wooden wheels pulled across the floors of attics. She wanted to paint old toys—antiquated trucks and trains and jack-in-the-boxes, dusty rocking horses and glass-eyed dolls with cracking faces. Abandoned toys that might come to life in some dark moment and whisper secrets too evil for human tongues. She could see the painting, done in grays. The doll's mouth, a clown's hat, the frightened eye of the rocking horse—these alone in red. A grim picture, horrifying in its message.

"Is it just me, or is there something wrong in that house?" she asked the steering wheel.

"It's you, it's you . . ." the squeak whined monotonously. "Crazy, crazy, crazy. . ."

Bo glanced at the sky and realized that she couldn't see the sun. Only an amorphous sphere of light beyond a curtain of haze. Dampness. Ooze. Everywhere.

She wasn't going to be able to keep it together much longer. She had to get home.

"Return, 12:45 P.M. But you just rented the car this morning," the clerk at the rental car counter noted.

Bo ran her tongue slowly over her upper teeth. "Thank you. I'm aware of that. *Your* job is to be aware that I'm *returning* the car."

"Just sign here," the young woman replied edgily. In her uniform she looked oddly like the clerk at Jamail's. Maybe a sister. Or maybe the same person working two jobs?

It happened frequently. People seeming to be other people, as if individuality were merely a tactical disguise beneath which the same personalities might hide. Anywhere. Everywhere. Over and over. In a full-blown mania, Bo recalled with chagrin, a stranger in a parking lot might be her barely remembered first-grade piano teacher. Or a UPS deliveryman the priest who had buried her sister. The thing was to keep it to yourself. Not run toward complete strangers yelling, "Mrs. Doonan? Father Ondek? Oh, I'm sorry, but you looked so much like . . ."

Lois Bittner hadn't been able to explain it.

"Who knows?" she had said with a shrug. "Maybe just a psychological mechanism. Your psyche is on overload from too much stimulation, and so you create comforting, familiar faces. Or else in that hyperaware state you're picking up things about strangers that really are identical to people you've known, and so you perceive them as looking identical. Who knows? Just remember to keep quiet about it. Reality is that strangers are just strangers. Leave it at that."

The plane wouldn't board for half an hour. Bo wandered into an airport gift shop, drawn by attractive displays arranged and illuminated to produce precisely this effect. Well, maybe not quite this effect, Bo thought. The little room gleamed. Colors clamored for attention from the covers of magazines and paperbacks. A rack of candy, pin-lighted from above, promised toothsome ecstasy. Bo tried on a ten-gallon hat and admired herself in a strategically placed mirror. She looked terrific, an Irish cowgirl. With a hand-crafted feather band, the hat would come only to $238.

Just the thing to wear to court, you lunatic. Get out of here before you buy electric pencil sharpeners shaped like armadillos for everybody at the office.

Lois Bittner had told Bo of a man, another manic-depressive, who'd bought Waterford wine decanters costing over half his annual salary for everyone on the faculty at the junior college where he taught Introduction to Accounting. That the man didn't even know most of his fellow instructors was irrelevant. Bo could understand. It was that wild, intense, I-love-everything feeling that came just before things went into warp speed. Just before slipping over into that realm of ominous insight where poisoned trees might glow with radiation from acid rains unleashed by murderous corporations and their puppet politicians. Where nobody would listen and the pain of ceaseless awareness could render you mute and frozen. Paranoid. Catatonic. But not quite.

Bo kept to herself the fact that not once had her "delusions" been anything but an amplified truth that normal people could deny, buffer, filter down to tolerable levels.

"Manic-depressives just lose the ability to ignore," Dr. Bittner had explained to her. "The world might be a very different place," she mused once, gazing out her office window at a bleak February afternoon, "if everybody lost that ability just a little bit."

Bo bought an armload of Houston newspapers and loped away from the gift shop as though it were the gateway to hell, then deliberately took a wrong turn that would provide fifteen minutes of brisk airport hiking until it was time to board the plane. The exercise would help, and nobody would find the notion of a woman dashing through airport corridors even remotely strange. Everybody dashed in airports. Even those who weren't running from madness.

"Please direct your attention to the video screens for a brief explanation of our safety procedures," the cabin attendant urged over the plane's PA system after Bo had boarded and found her seat. No one paid the slightest attention, including Bo. If the plane crashed, they'd all be dead anyway. The plane's safety equipment, flotation devices, and emergency exits would be discovered to be jammed, dysfunctional, and not inspected since the craft's maiden flight in 1983. Bo could hear the eleven o'clock news report. "... investigation of the tragic October airline disaster that claimed 158 lives revealed today that safety mechanisms that might have saved half the doomed passengers failed to operate . . ." It was just a fact of life. Bo found it comforting that for once everybody else knew the truth too.

After the plane forced itself off the ground, Bo opened Weppo's case file on her tray table. On a clean narrative sheet she wrote what she knew so far.

"Four-year-old deaf boy is found tied up in a mountain shack. He has had no ASL training, but somebody has taught him to say his name, which comes out like Weppo. He's smart; I'm sure of it. He hasn't been starved or abused, but he's very pale. (Kept indoors somewhere?) Whoever brought him to the shack and tied him to the mattress fed him SpaghettiOs and built a fire to keep him warm before leaving him alone there. Whoever it was probably tied him to the mattress to keep him from running away. Whoever it was *intended* to come back, but didn't.

"Annie Garcia remembered the license number of a car she saw. A car stolen in Houston and found in San Diego with a dead drug addict in it. I found a grocery receipt from a Houston grocery where the car was parked. This can't be sheer coincidence. The receipt must have fallen out of the car. This would mean that the dead druggie stole the car in Houston, bought the SpaghettiOs in Houston, has something to do with the Rowes since he used their account to charge the food at Jamail's, and is the one who left Weppo to die in that shack. Except he didn't mean to leave him to die. Then what *did* he mean? To go down into San Diego and get drugs and then come back? Maybe.

"So who is this dead guy? Maybe a servant, handyman, driver for the Rowes? Did he kidnap Weppo from the wealthy family?

"And who is the child in the old Rowe photographs? A relative, obviously, unless I imagined it. A relative the little boy has replicated genetically. But why wouldn't the influential Rowes have notified the police, the media, if a child related to them had been kidnapped?"

Wait a minute! Maybe they did.

Clambering over a couple who looked eerily like Roy Rogers and Dale Evans, Bo headed for the in-flight phone on the wall between cabins. Sometimes the police got gag orders for the media in kidnapping cases. And any judge would have seen the merit in a gag order for this case. With the state senate election in three days, a gag would save the state of Texas the expense of a second election after Yannick's people claimed media coverage of a Rowe kidnapping threw the close election to Tia.

Remembering the billboard eyes, Bo was stunned by another thought. What if Tia Rowe staged the kidnapping in order to get miles of free media just before the election? Bo knew a soulless psychopath when she saw one. Those charming, manipulative characters incapable of anything but self-interest. Tia Rowe was one of them, Bo would have bet on it.

"Houston Police Department," a young male voice answered briskly. "Desk Sergeant Tromley."

Bo dropped her voice an octave.

"I've got some information on the Rowe kidnapping," she whispered. "Let me talk to the investigating officer."

If a kidnapping had been reported, the HPD would be set up to receive precisely this sort of call.

"What?" the voice replied.

"The kidnapped Rowe Child."

"Rowe? Just a minute..."

Bo could hear the desk sergeant talking to someone else in the background.

"Something about a kidnapped Rowe child...?"

"It's just some loony," the older voice responded. "The Rowe kids're grown. One of 'em's—"

Bo hung up quickly. Whoever Weppo was, his absence from Houston had not been reported to the Houston police.

Roy and Dale were, uncharacteristically, poring over a racing form as Bo returned to her seat.

"Happy trails," she murmured.

Roy appeared puzzled.

"I think Happy Trails is in the third race at Belmont," Dale explained cheerfully.

"Thanks for the tip." Roy grinned.

Bo buried herself in the newspapers she'd bought at the airport. They all told the same story. Tia Rowe, wife of shipping heir MacLaren Rowe, was in a closely contested race for a senatorial seat vacated two months ago. Rowe's opponent, Bea Yannick, was a Catholic grandmother of four, widowed when her oil-exec husband was transferred to Houston from the family enclave in Pennsylvania during the boom, and promptly dropped dead. Yannick had stayed, raised seven kids alone, gone to law school, chaired the school board, and launched an unsuccessful campaign to introduce the notion of zoning to Houston. The attempt, Yannick said, was prompted by the existence of a thriving massage parlor and drug dealership across the street from a public school attended by two of her grandchildren. The media coverage suggested that Yannick was a gutsy Yankee who, while well liked, couldn't overcome the aristocratic Rowe name.

A counterculture paper called *The Bayou Banner* gave a different picture. Tia Rowe, according to an investigative reporter named Gretchen Tally, was a conniving egotist whose campaign platform had a designer label and no substance whatever. Without violating the strictures of good journalism Tally managed to suggest that a financially distressed society matron known more for catered brunches than informed opinions might find the temptations of political power overwhelming. Hadn't a Big Bend mining consortium already under attack by environmental groups contributed generously to the Rowe campaign? And what about Tia's sudden friendship with the wife of the president of a paper conglomerate methodically denuding central Texas of its few remaining forests? The widely publicized "future" of a Rowe win in the senate, the radical reporter suggested, would be Tia Rowe's, not Texas's. Bo sensed that Tally was on to something, and fought her way over the beaming couple to make one more phone call.

"Tally's not in," a traditionally cranky editor snarled. "Wanna leave a message?"

"I've got something on Tia Rowe that may interest her," Bo announced. "A Rowe child, victim of an attempted murder yesterday in California." Bo gave both her home and office numbers and hung up. The message had been tantalizing enough to ensure a return call from the most jaded newshound.

"Attempted murder by two men in hospital." Bo completed her chronology of events surrounding the child. It was the piece that didn't fit.

For the rest of the flight Bo nursed a series of canned fruit juices that tasted more like cans than juice, and stared out the window. No slowing the racing thoughts now. Might as well watch clouds. She was ahead of the lithium by weeks. It would kick in eventually when it built up to blood level, but what would happen in the meantime?

Maybe Weppo might actually be safe in the confidential foster home Madge would have selected for him by now. A foster home licensed for secrecy, for the protection of children whose parents were violent, predatory, criminal. Bo pretended to believe that a system with thousands of employees and a computer network accessible to seven other agencies could keep Weppo's whereabouts a secret. She had to believe it, had to let go of the little boy. If she didn't, what lay ahead for her would almost certainly involve nightmarish mental disintegration, a psychiatric hospitalization, the loss of her job.

A bag lady stared back at her from her own reflection in the scratched airplane window. Mad, ruined, incoherent. That terror was always there. Would always be there.

"No way!" she resolved fiercely. She'd get home, check in with the shrink at the clinic, get a couple of sedatives, go home and sleep.

A call to Bill Denny's unit at the SDPD would put the cops on the trail of the Rowe connection, if there really was one. If she wasn't imagining the whole thing.

Bo bit the knuckle of an index finger and felt the plane's wheels scrape tarmac. Home. But, a thundering unease told her, not home free.

17

Chivas, Messy

In Houston the bartender at Oak Arbor called the cab to remove Mac Rowe from the club's paneled premises earlier than usual. The tennis crowd wouldn't begin drifting in until around 3:30, and it was always necessary to shovel Mac into a cab before he outraged the club's matrons by urinating into one of their Gucci bags again. Mac looked bad today. Not just wild-eyed and dirty, but sick. Really sick. Bruised and yellowish around the eyes and under the fingernails. The barkeep had seen it before. In that line of work you saw what the amber liquids lined up behind the bar could do. A slow poison. In spite of himself he felt sorry for Mac Rowe.

Mac felt a similar pity when he got home. He'd managed to stagger from the cab into the house only to find Tia gone and that idiot of a new maid sniveling something about being sick. The pain in his gut was like a rivet gun, hot as hell.

"Gimme my pills, damn you!" he roared at the stupid creature. But she just trembled and snuffled.

"Ah cain't unner*stan'* ya, Mistah Rowe! *What* you want?"

Deely would have known. Would have been standing at

94

the door with the pills. Mac stumbled at the edge of the hall rug and fell against the table. Who in hell had put a *spittoon* full of flowers in his hall? He threw the brass container against the door in a shower of leaded-glass splinters.

"Mistah *Rowe . . . !*" the girl sniveled.

Where was Deely? He had to find Deely. She'd give him the pills. The pain would stop. Probably up in the attic with the family secret, his idiot grandson.

"*Deely . . . ?*" he screamed and grabbed in both hands the curving banister he'd slid down as a child. She'd be up there. She was always up there.

"Deely ain't here no mo' . . ." the whine intruded. "And I got to leave now, go to the doctor . . ."

"Get out!" Mac Rowe bellowed hoarsely. He wanted to pull out a stair rail and beat the girl into silence, but the rails wouldn't break loose. Behind him a last shard of leaded glass fell and shattered as the door closed. The creature was gone. Now where was Deely?

On all fours Mac made it to the first landing of the curved staircase his mother had descended for her wedding in imported *peau de soie* and lace mitts. She'd carried a white parasol. Mac could see the picture in his mind as his bowels writhed and then exploded. The pain was white-hot, ramming his guts out, climbing his throat. He fell with his face wedged between two banisters, and couldn't move. From his mouth and nose something warm gurgled and dripped in thin, red strings down a wall of faded photographs.

The last word Mac Rowe would pronounce was "fuck," but nobody heard.

MacLaren Rowe was dead.

18

Message from Houston

Deely saw the pirogue cutting through bayou mist before she could see who was in it. Her hand tightened on the 12-gauge shotgun resting across her lap. Both barrels were loaded, and she'd known how to shoot since she'd weighed enough to stay on her feet with the recoil. It was probably Raveneau in the hollow-log boat he'd bought from a Cajun. If not, an intruder would find access to the shack on its stilts above murky swamp water impossible. There was only one way in—up a rope ladder lashed to the narrow porch. And that way was guarded by a two-hundred-pound woman possessed of strong beliefs and a loaded gun.

"Allo!" Raveneau's voice barely penetrated the moist afternoon air. *"C'est votre* nephew, Raveneau! Don't shoot!"

Deely smiled. Raveneau had hung around with Cajuns so long he forgot to speak English half the time. The pirogue slipped silently under the shack and soon the young man's huge coffee-colored hands were seen gripping the ladder. His eyes were solemn.

"What's happened? Did you hear from Marguerite?" Deely had to know.

"She called Mama 'bout two hours ago," he answered swiftly. "Said a woman come to the door of the house there in Houston sayin' somebody tried to kill the boy out in California. Marguerite, she say she done run out the house and ain't goin' back. Said you to hear, you gotta call this woman in California, tell what you know. Mama sent me to carry you back."

Raveneau's mama was Marguerite's mama as well. And Deely Brasseur's sister. And she was right. Deely would have to tell somebody what she knew. The plan had failed.

Deely wanted to pray, but lowered herself to the pirogue instead. She'd pray on the way. Pray that it wasn't already too late.

19

Cross-Stitch

In the San Diego suburb of Alpine, Angela Reavey stabbed a needle in and out of linen fabric. It was a tablecloth, with a Christmas design in counted cross-stitch. Wreaths with holly berries and a Grecian key border in forest green. It was pretty. It would look nice on the table for Christmas dinner.

With a cuff of her sweatshirt she wiped away tears steaming her tortoiseshell glasses. Jennifer Martinelli would never see another Christmas. Never get another pretty gift tied in ribbons. Jennifer would never read Laura Ingalls Wilder books or try out for cheerleader or have a boyfriend.

Angela blinked at her watch. It was over. The broken little body was buried by now, the funeral complete, the mourners and the media gone. In a pile of flowers left by the mortician atop the fresh grave would be a nosegay of pink rosebuds. Angela had ordered the nosegay. It was the one she imagined Jennifer might have been given for her first dance.

In the mirror over the fireplace Angela Reavey regarded herself. A plump, red-eyed woman in her husband's sweatshirt.

Kind. Ordinary. A social worker. Not the sort of woman who relished the power of life-and-death decisions involving children.

She'd asked Ben to take the kids out somewhere for the afternoon, to leave her alone during the time of the funeral. It was essential, this quiet, thoughtful time alone. She needed to finish grieving for the child who was only one of hundreds whose case files would lie for a time on her desk.

But this one had died. This one had been killed.

Maybe she could have prevented the tragedy. And maybe not. But she would never forget Jennifer Martinelli.

The sound of a car in the drive disturbed her reverie. Ben home early, but where were the kids?

Then a polite knock at the door.

Angela tugged the sweatshirt over her hips and answered. Two men in cowboy hats stood in the breezeway.

"We're from the *Dallas Times,* ma'am," the larger one drawled. "Our paper's doing some articles on child abuse, and—"

"You'll have to talk to somebody in public relations," Angela recited. "It's DSS policy. I can't talk to you."

There had been several phone calls from reporters, especially yesterday after the hearing over at St. Mary's and Andrew LaMarche's incendiary comments. But no reporters had come to the house.

The shorter, thinner man placed a toe of his boot deliberately between the door and the frame. Angela noticed that the toe was capped with dull, thick metal. She couldn't close the door on it, but at least the chain lock was still on.

"Now!" the skinny one snarled, and the big one rammed his shoulder against the open door. The chain lock snapped loose easily and hung swinging from a splintered chunk of the white frame.

"You're gonna do us a little favor," the big one sneered, twisting Angela's wrist behind her back and then kicking her across the room into the TV on its portable stand. She felt the back of her head break the TV screen, but no pain as she slid to the floor.

"The tranquilizers," she thought. The tranquilizers the doctor had given her obliterated the pain.

"What do you want?" she wept.

They had guns. They were going to kill her.

"You know somebody named Bo Bradley?" the skinny man asked. He'd crossed the room and jammed the heel of his boot into her stomach. The gun in his hand had a black thing on the end that looked like a vacuum cleaner accessory. A silencer. It must be a silencer. They could kill her and the neighbors wouldn't hear the shots.

"She works over in court investigations," Angela whispered. "I don't know her."

The boot in her stomach gouged deeper, cutting off her breath. The other man wrapped a paw around her neck and pulled her to her feet.

"Get on that phone," he roared, "and find out where the fuck the dummy kid is. It's Bradley's case. You work for the same outfit. You can find out. Do it!"

Angela felt herself propelled again, pushed, dragged, her arms breaking. The phone was rammed against her right ear, a gun in her left.

"I can't . . . I don't know what you're talking about," she sobbed.

"A dummy kid, a boy. He was in St. Mary's Hospital. It was Bradley's case. Find out where the fuck he is!"

The bearlike man thundered into the kitchen and pulled the receiver of the kitchen extension its full length to the arched dining room doorway. "Don't fuck around," he warned. "I can hear you."

The other man stood behind her, pressed against her with

the gun in her ear and the thumb of his right hand gouging up, under her breastbone. The pain was deadly.

"Do it!" he insisted. "Now!"

She could feel the urgent, angry wiriness of him. His hatred. His fear. In his body she felt the absolute certainty that he would kill her if she failed to comply.

Angela Reavey had not known before the feel of a killer. Her mind shut down, faded to a mere buzz inside her skull. Then something fierce took over. Survival. They were going to kill her if she didn't do what they said. With numb fingers she dialed St. Mary's Hospital.

"Discharge information, please . . ."

The high, husky voice was one she'd never heard, coming from her own mouth.

"This is Angela Reavey with Child Protective Services . . .

"Yes. My worker number is 17-262. I need the placement address for a child discharged from St. Mary's today to the custody of CPS. Bo Bradley did the initial investigation. Her name will be on the chart.

"Yes, I know this is a confidential placement, but there were medical complications and the Department of Social Services has ordered the Medi-Cal documentation hand-delivered to the foster home today to prevent interruption in care when the child is seen by a private physician on Monday. The CPS placement office is closed on Saturday. I need the address.

"Forty-nine seventeen Bayard in Pacific Beach? The Chandlers. Thank you."

Angela Reavey felt the man's left arm stretch into the air, smelled the acrid odor of his sweat, and then the weight of the gun smashed into the base of her skull.

20

A Voice on the Answering Machine

After retrieving her car from the palm-swaying airport parking lot, Bo forced herself to stop at the university's twenty-four-hour psychiatric clinic for sedatives powerful enough to knock her out. It was difficult to sit still. She'd paced outside the pharmacy until five o'clock, waiting for the stupid pills. But it was going to be okay. She'd get home, jog, soak in a hot bath, pop a sedative, and crash. There was no other way. Nothing else she *could* do, if she wanted to avoid an unscheduled vacation in hell.

The answering machine was blinking in the gloom as Bo got home, kicked off her boots, and snapped the deadbolt. Her apartment was musty, but opening the windows seemed reckless under the circumstances. Even turning on a light seemed suicidal. People with poisoned guns might be watching. Two men coldly determined to murder a helpless child. Two men who had murdered an orderly because he got in their way. Bo watched the throbbing light. Whoever the men were, they would undoubtedly meet any standard criteria for sanity, while she would not. A fact of life.

Ignore the phone. Stay away from the whole mess. Take care of yourself!

With exaggerated deliberation Bo padded into the bathroom and ran hot water into the tub. Through the steam the transparent bubbles looked like mouths trying to scream, producing only silence. Bo threw a handful of sage leaves into the water and breathed deeply. The scent brought a momentary calm as she peeled off a costume donned three thousand miles ago, and sank gratefully into the hot water.

Killers, hell-bent on murdering Weppo. Who were they? What did they have to do with this cold-eyed Texas politician and her appalling taste in interior decorating? Hadn't LaMarche said they shot at Weppo with a Smith & Wesson .38? What in hell was a Smith & Wesson .38? It sounded Western. Bo imagined the guns wielded by Roy Rogers, Gene Autry, the cowboy heroes of her first movies. Splendid, silver guns pulled from chrome-studded holsters to shoot unshaven villains in black hats from the balconies of saloons. The villains, she knew even then, were stuntmen who fell onto mattresses below camera range. And where was the mattress for Weppo, who wasn't even a villain? Just a deaf kid, like Laurie. A live deaf kid, unlike Laurie. Through the open bathroom door Bo could see a faint, pink pulse from the blinking answering machine light.

"Now, now, now," it demanded.

She couldn't ignore it.

"Bo, it's Es," the first message chirped as Bo toweled her dripping hair over the machine. "You must be asleep. I'm going to bed too. Mildred's fine; she's shedding all over Henry's favorite chair as I speak, and Madge is handling the confidential placement for the kid. Call me when you wake up, okay?"

The second message was quintessential Madge Aldenhoven, the soul of efficiency. "Bo? It's Madge. This case is too complex for handling at our level. I've arranged the foster care placement. CPS will monitor, but make no contact with the child until the police have done their work. It's too dangerous. In fact you are to have no further involvement with this case. I hope I've made this clear, Bo. My decision is in your best interest, and the child's. See you Monday."

Too late, Madge. The message would have been recorded as the plane flew toward Houston. A million years ago.

In the bedroom Bo pulled on her favorite sweats, teal blue with Mayan symbols on the sleeves. The answering machine clicked and buzzed to the next message. A strange voice. Unfamiliar. Weeping. Through the damp hood of Bo's sweatshirt the voice was muffled, the words indecipherable. A voice from some netherworld. Bo shivered, marshaled her thoughts.

There are no voices from the grave, Bradley. It's not Laurie. It's not even Caillech Bera; she'd moan in Gaelic, not English.

Shakily Bo punched the rewind and then the playback. Madge's message again. "See you on Monday." And then the other.

"My name is Delilah Brasseur," it keened at contralto level. A rich, deep female voice. Tremulous with emotion. "Until two weeks ago I was the housekeeper for the Rowes. I know about the baby, the little boy." Here the voice broke in a silence so intense even the plastic tape captured it. "I don't know who you are," Delilah Brasseur sobbed now, "but don't let nothin' happen to my baby! I called the daddy to come get him, an' he did, but if somebody tried to kill the child out there, that mean the daddy already come to harm. There's danger! So much danger it can't be told! Get the baby and get him somewheres where ain't nobody know you at, till Tuesday. Then it be over. I cain't call the police, cain't do nothin' more. It up to you, lady, whoever you be. You got to trust me, do as I says! Please! It all up to you!''

Here the tape clicked off and over to automatic rewind. In its hum Bo heard the final sentence echo and echo.

"It all up to you . . . up to you . . . you, you, you."

She could hear nothing else.

In her purse lay a plastic pharmacy bottle containing the tranquilizing drug that would let her sleep, make her sleep until the middle of tomorrow. The drug that would allow her body to rest and fight to restore some balance to the skewed chemical battle raging in her skull. With that help and a few days of disciplined quiet, she might make it through. Might avoid the hospital, the locked doors, the cement-walled "garden" where you could pace and smoke. There was always a "garden." It never had flowers.

"Reality, there's nothing but reality," Bo pronounced solemnly. But what was it? Maybe she'd imagined the message on the tape. Maybe it wasn't there at all. No "Delilah Brasseur." No clear, uncompromising instructions. Just the quiet hiss of blank tape.

Bo knew as a personal catechism the difference between manic-depression and schizophrenia. Both were hell, but one could involve audial delusions—hearing voices produced from within one's own brain, but seeming to come from outside. She'd seen it. Other patients, hospitalized, hearing voices from unplugged TVs, silent radios, blank tape recordings. As a young woman struggling to make sense of psychiatric chaos, she'd believed for a while that those suffering from voices must be picking up the thousand invisible radio waves webbing the air. Maybe in the fillings of their teeth. Something. But she didn't believe it anymore. There was no explanation yet for the tormenting voices of schizophrenia. Nobody really knew where they came from. Or why they came. What Bo knew was that she wasn't schizophrenic. Never heard voices. Never would. Which would mean that the message on the recording was real.

She pushed the playback button again. Estrella, Madge, and Delilah Brasseur. It was *there*.

"Get the baby and get him somewheres where ain't nobody know you at . . ."

She played it again. And then again. A black woman. Mature. Frightened. But deeply courageous. In the voice Bo could hear a resonance of valor, the steel edge of a desperate decision made with finality. That decision had been to call Bo!

The tinny buzz was back. Like twin metallic mosquitoes living in her ears. The countertop, her pottery dishes, a Mexican sugar bowl purchased whimsically for the ant imbedded in its glaze—all seemed strange. Temporal. Fake. Vaguely familiar, but not really what they seemed. Not substantial, as if they might vanish at any moment, or turn into something else. And it wouldn't matter. Nothing mattered, except the message.

". . . get him somewheres where ain't nobody know you at . . ."

Wandering aimlessly through her own apartment, now a landscape of objects retreating from their functional definitions, Bo called up the ghost of Lois Bittner from her mind. The imaginary conversation. Favorite gimmick of Gestalt therapists everywhere. Bo had chatted with more empty armchairs in Bittner's office than she cared to count.

Fixing her attention on one of the two pine barstools regrettably whitewashed during a Taos period, she imagined the petite psychiatrist perched on it, regarding Bo quizzically.

"You say a total stranger left a message on your answering machine directing you to abandon self-preservation and run away in order to save a deaf child from some wholly incomprehensible danger?"

"It's not running away," Bo answered aloud. "It's not running away from anything..."

"A deaf child?... a danger you know to be real but can't understand? Doesn't that sound like Laurie? Like her depression for which you always blamed yourself, because you felt that you abandoned her?"

"I know Laurie's depression wasn't my fault. She was a depressive. Another version of the weird brain chemistry I've got, Grandma O'Reilly had, and that great-uncle in Ireland who spent thirty years writing a poetic history of the wee people in McGillicuddy's Reeks and then hanged himself in Derrynane Abbey. I know! But this is different..."

"How is this different?"

"This is real..."

The ghost of Lois Bittner looked pointedly over the top of half glasses.

"Real," she enunciated with precision, "is only what you think it is!"

Something was wrong. Lois Bittner had never said that. The eminently practical psychiatrist never hinted that reality might be fungible, having aspects that could replace one another as two nickels might replace a dime.

Bo stared at the empty barstool. She'd known it all along. Only framed it in Bittner's accent to give the notion authority, credibility. Her reactions to this case, to the little boy, were certainly colored by Laurie. Laurie's tortured life from which Bo had fled. Embarrassed. Ashamed.

But there was something else. Some pattern plaited with wisps of fog, penned invisibly across a clutter of events and people. Just a glyph, an occasional whole word drifting into sight at random. A grocery receipt, a Texas politician, a little boy learning that red has a name.

Bo could taste the pattern with her bones. All around her, in her.

"It's the sight," her grandmother's voice insisted.

"Something like that," Bo acknowledged.

And she would have to choose. Delilah Brasseur's urgent instructions, or the correctly prescribed capsules waiting in her purse. Self-preservation or a part in a deadly drama that could only be described, metaphorically and realistically, as madness.

Bo sifted her mind for answers and instead found images. Laurie at Cape Cod, screaming in the wind. Mark holding a baby that was not hers. Weppo, his huge, burnt-sugar eyes calling to her from a world of silence at the edge of a small grave.

"No!"

The word rose up in her, a torrent of certainty that rattled the furniture, echoed beyond the walls and out over the sea.

She might be crazy, was crazy by any standard definition, but beneath it all she was still Barbara Joan Bradley whose deaf little sister had named her Bo. And Bo Bradley would not walk away from reality, ever again. *Her* reality, no one else's. It might be skewed, but it was the only reality she had. And in it was a little boy with almost no time left.

21

"There Is Dust from the Whirlwind"
—Paiute chant by Wovoka

Four thousand feet above the desert floor, the Sierra Nevada purple at her back, Annie Garcia stood silent in her grandson's yard. She was watching the sky dance. Watching color shift from magenta to lavender to gray. Sunsets came early to the land her people claimed. A land far from the cities, hidden between the Sierra and Inyo Mountains.

Chilled, she turned to go inside, but something was happening in the sky. From the distant desert, spirals of alkaline dust twisted upward, writhing like snakes trying to walk upright. A visual contortion of light and dust. It was the whirlwind!

"Grandmother," Charlie Garcia called respectfully from the door behind her, "it's getting cold. Come inside."

Annie allowed her gaze to linger briefly on the dust clouds. They climbed and fell, joined and collapsed, tore at the sky with their urgency. The spirits, again. Rising up cloaked in dust to shout messages no one could comprehend except the shamans.

Annie was no shaman. But she had an idea what it was

109

all about. Hadn't the spirits been giving her signs for two days now? Always about the child. And the white woman who had no children and said she was loco. This whirlwind was a warning, about them. A warning thrown up from the desert to the south, toward San Diego. They were in danger, the two of them. Annie knew it. But what could she do up here, six hundred miles away?

Walking thoughtfully toward the house, she pointed to the sky.

"The whirlwind," she stated.

Charlie nodded somberly. "But what does it mean? It is Nu'mi/na'a?"

Annie sighed. It was difficult, being an old woman with a grandson who'd gone off to college in New Mexico and come back more "Indian" than any Paiute Annie'd ever known. Charlie, who had been named for her husband, was a member of the tribal council and the area intertribal council. He'd worked in Los Angeles long enough to save money, and then bought a gas station here in Lone Pine, married a Shoshone woman, and settled permanently. Charlie didn't drink. He was waiting to be old enough to become a singer. Being Paiute was his life, he said. And that meant he expected his grandmother, as an old one, to know everything.

"There is a child," Annie began, "who can't hear..."

"Wait," Charlie Garcia cautioned as he helped her into the house. "Everyone should know about this."

In the steamy kitchen Annie enjoyed a plate of fry-bread with honey as Charlie gathered people out of the woodwork. Within minutes fifteen Indians, all visiting for the pow-wow celebrating Charlie's daughter's first menstruation and entry into womanhood, were gathered in the warm room.

Annie surveyed the collection of plaid shirts, the wide bronze faces, and chuckled. She felt good, not sick at all.

Maybe she'd been wrong about the cry-dance. Maybe she wasn't going to die after all.

"There is a child," Annie explained slowly, "who is in great danger."

Everyone was listening. It would be a good story.

22

Bach, a Sedative, and Seven-Grain Bread

Bo selected a tape—Bach's Toccata and Fugue in C—and then hit the eject button. The sonorous organ was too religious.

You're not the flaming Virgin Mother, Bradley. Cool it.

One of the Brandenburgs would be better. Less likely to create the additional burden of a halo around her already throbbing head. Grabbing a random Brandenburg, she stuffed it into the cassette deck and attempted to arrange her thoughts in time with the music.

"Get Weppo and go someplace," she chanted with the Baroque chords.

But where? And what would that involve?

Buses and trains were too slow. She was sure of that. But too slow for what? A plane. Too risky, too easy to trace even if she used an assumed name. Weppo would be noticeable and so, unfortunately, would she.

"Oh, you mean the deaf-mute kid and the lunatic red-head? Sure. They got on Flight 89 for Denver." Bo could

112

hear the ticket agent explaining her whereabouts to anyone who asked.

And what was the penalty in California for kidnapping? Bo saw herself in the dock, handcuffed, wearing a white choir robe as bewigged barristers argued that this case represented the single instance in the entire history of American jurisprudence in which the insanity defense might justifiably be employed. Except American lawyers didn't have wigs, and why was she wearing a choir robe?

Something clanged over the music. The phone. The phone was ringing. Bo watched it, but didn't answer. After four rings the machine clicked on.

Madge's voice, strung tight as a violin string.

"Bo, something's happened."

No kidding, Madge! Thanks for sharing that.

Madge seemed to be choosing every word from a dictionary before pronouncing it. A slow narration. On the wrong speed.

"Angela Reavey has been attacked. Her husband and children came home and found her only minutes ago. She was apparently beaten and hit over the head. She's still alive, but there's some question about whether she'll make it. They're on the way to the hospital in an ambulance now."

There was a brief pause.

"I don't know why, but I think there's some connection to your Johnny Doe. I'm calling to tell you, don't stay there! If you come home, leave! Go over to Estrella's, or go to a motel. The department will pay for it.

"And call me."

Madge hung up as Bo went into overdrive.

Angela Reavey? Angela Reavey wasn't involved in Weppo's case at any level. Reavey worked over in reunification, in the back end, assessing the point at which families were rehabilitated and ready to retrieve kids from foster care. Why would killers go after Reavey?

Bo let her eyes roam jerkily about the room as she thought. Barstools. Navajo rug. Her boots, kicked off when she came in the door. The clump of newspapers she'd bought in Houston and mindlessly carried from the plane to the car, and from the car into the apartment.

Newspapers!

That was it. Angela Reavey's name had been all over the papers because of the Martinelli case. Anybody, literally anybody, could know that Reavey worked for Child Protective Services. And anybody who didn't work for Child Protective Services wouldn't know the system's intricacies. Wouldn't know... but wait. Reavey would have an identification number, just like any other CPS worker. With it, she could get information on any case, and child, in the system.

Bo took deep breaths and released them slowly. Then she moved toward the phone.

The killers had gone to Angela Reavey to find out where Weppo was. Beaten her. Had she told them? Bo tried to remember Angela Reavey, and couldn't. Most of the back end workers were motherly types. They spent a lot of time with the kids in foster care. Nice people. Social workers. Could one of them stand up to brutality, torture, the threat of death?

Bo dialed St. Mary's Hospital and reminded herself to speak slowly.

"Discharge desk? This is Bo Bradley. My number is 20-035. I'm calling about a Johnny Doe on my caseload released today—"

"Yes, Ms. Bradley," the clerk interrupted. "We know about the Medi-Cal documentation. Ms. Reavey phoned just a little while ago. It's all taken care of."

"What Medi-Cal documentation? What in bloody hell are

you talking about? Did you give Reavey the address of the foster home where my kid is?''

Bo could feel rivers of rage in her arms and hands.

''Yes, but I'm afraid I can't give you that information . . .''

The clerk, nervous, was falling back on the stubborn nasality known to every lower-echelon member of every bureaucratic system in the Western world. Bo would happily have broken the nose through which the woman continued to whine.

''There's a memo in the computer. It's flagged from a, uh, Marge Alderhaven, that Bo Bradley is to get no information . . .''

''You will die slowly from a rare and disfiguring gum disease,'' Bo promised the woman, ''and nobody will come to your funeral!''

Bo slammed the phone onto the machine and sent a chip of its beige plastic flying into the sink.

How was she going to find out what the killers already knew? Who would tell her where Weppo was? Not the hospital. Not Madge. What about the police? They could get there in time, with sirens. They could save Weppo, if she could not.

''Let me speak to Bill Denny,'' Bo said after dialing the San Diego Police Department number.

''Denny's not in. Shift's over. Could I connect you to someone else in his unit?''

''No. Yes. I guess so. But hurry!''

''Homicide,'' a casual voice answered. ''Detective Gottleib.''

''This is Bo Bradley at CPS. Somebody's going to kill a kid, the one that got shot at last night at St. Mary's Hospital. They're on their way to the foster home, the killers I mean. *Now!* You've got to send squad cars. Use sirens . . .''

"I know the case," Gottleib acknowledged. "Bill Denny's. Or at least it *was* Denny's. I think it's being reassigned . . ."

"Please listen to me," Bo tried to speak softly. She was shaking, shuddering. "There's very little time. Call St. Mary's and find out where the foster home is. They'll tell the police. Then you need to send a SWAT team immediately."

It was hopeless. Even if Gottleib followed up, it would be half an hour before he could make all the phone calls necessary to confirm what she'd said. And in a half hour Weppo could be as still and lifeless as Laurie.

"It up to you . . ." Delilah Brasseur's words echoed inside the music flooding the room. "You, you, you . . ."

Bo knotted her fists and sobbed. She wanted to smash everything in her apartment, gouge out the walls, kick the entire building piece by piece into the sea.

But the Bach was there, melodic, repetitive, precise. The music traveled along her arteries like smoke. Calming, but insistent.

"Either calm down," it prompted, "or plan what to wear to the boy's funeral."

Pouring three-fourths of the powder from one of the capsules into the sink, Bo swallowed what was left in the open end with gulps of water. On an empty stomach the effect was almost immediate.

The tremors subsided. Her rage went from boil to simmer. She could think a little.

Empty stomach. Eat something or you'll throw up.

A bag of seven-grain bread bought in a rare moment of health consciousness lay on the counter. Bo seized a slice and wolfed it, pacing.

How could she find out where Weppo was? Who would tell her?

Bo ran through the sequence of people who would know. Madge. The discharge clerk. Bill Denny. Useless. There was a conspiracy to keep her away from Weppo. A conspiracy that would ensure his death.

She could see his huge eyes pleading with her, as they'd done in the hospital when he made the beer-drinking sign and then threw the cup òn the floor, angering the nurse.

The nurse!

A last chance, and a feeble one. But a chance.

"I'd like to talk to the charge nurse who was on yesterday morning," Bo told the third-floor nursing student who answered. "I don't remember her name, but she offered to lend me some books, and I'm really interested . . . Uh, this is Barbara O'Reilly. I work for Child Protective Services. You know . . ."

The use of her childhood name carried a ring of honesty while avoiding immediate recognition.

"Sure," the student nurse replied. "That's Susan Cooper. She's always reading those religious books. Her home number's 570-5782."

"Thanks," Bo said carefully, and hung up.

Susan Cooper was overjoyed at Bo's change of heart.

"God works in mysterious ways," she murmured. "I just knew when I saw you looking at Dr. Hinckle's book yesterday morning that you were special."

In the length of time it took Susan Cooper to pronounce "special," Bo could have retiled the kitchen.

"Well, I thought about Dr. Hinckle, working on this case," Bo sing-songed, replicating Cooper's inflection. "You know, I sometimes feel a need for guidance, seeing all these poor children . . ."

"Oh, I'm *sure* you do! And that *sweet* little deaf boy—how's he doing?"

Nurse Sailboat didn't know Bo was off the case. This was it. The one chance.

"A *wonderful* foster home," Bo twittered. "Such *loving,*

caring, people! Did you get to meet them when they came to get Weppo?''

"The Chandlers? I sure did! They came right before my shift was over at 3:30. They seemed so nice."

Bo tried to remember to breathe, and went for the goal.

"A lovely home too. I was so glad that Weppo would get to be close to . . . you know . . ."

"The beach? Yes, that'll be a treat for the little guy, and there' s that fabulous ice cream place right on Garnet . . ."

Garnet—that meant Pacific Beach.

Bo replaced the receiver and checked her purse. Lithium. Sedatives. She stuffed the seven-grain bread on top of the drugs with one hand, and found the Cs in the phone book with the other. Richard and Caroline Chandler lived at forty-nine seventeen Bayard in Pacific Beach. One beach community north of Bo, a five-minute drive.

Bo hit the door running. She might just make it. There might be just enough time.

23

Estrella

Estrella Benedict stroked the smooth fur of the fox terrier in her lap. Mildred was safe. But what to do about Bo? Surely Bo wasn't still asleep. She should have called by now.

Letting the dog have the brocade chair, Estrella rose to pace the length of her living room, again.

"We just got the carpet," her husband, Henry, remarked from the couch. "You're wearing a path."

"Cute," she replied. "*Muy lindo*. I'm worried about Bo. She hasn't called."

"So call her," Henry Benedict suggested.

"She won't answer, even if she's there. Not when she gets, you know, a little out of it. She just stays in that apartment and paints those Indian things, doesn't answer the phone. She says it's good for her."

"Then it's probably good for her."

A man of few words and clear ideas, Henry readjusted the sights on the rifle he'd just cleaned, and snapped it back in the gun rack inside a custom-made cabinet. He left the cabinet unlocked.

"Do you want to drive over there again?"

"No." Estrella sighed. "We were just there two hours ago. I didn't see her car. Maybe she's gone to a motel, like Madge said. But Madge never really talked to her, just left a message. I don't think Bo got the message about what happened to Angela Reavey. I know she'd call me. And she'd come to get Mildred. She'd never leave Mildred this long unless something was wrong."

"Madge'll call when they know more about Reavey," Henry pointed out the fourth time in an hour. "Until then there's nothing we can do but wait."

Henry Benedict hoped the men who had shot the child would come to his house looking for his wife's friend. He was ready. Earlier he'd surprised two Jehovah's Witnesses by shoving them off the porch with the screen door and then training a rifle on them as they sprawled on the lawn. Estrella knew she'd laugh at the scene later when she could describe it to Bo. The men had left a stack of little magazines and a Bible on the grass in their haste to retreat. Henry had bitten a plastic toothpick in half and spit the pieces on the lawn.

"*Damn,*" he'd sighed. "Wish it'd been the dirtbags that shot up the hospital."

"I'm going to call Madge," Estrella spoke directly to the new maroon carpeting under her feet.

"Madge's at the hospital with Reavey's supervisor. You know that," Henry, rather than the carpet, replied.

An elaborate beveled mirror over the fireplace, a wedding present from two aunts in Culiacán, reflected slices of the room. Estrella entertained the idea of breaking it over her husband's head. She had to do something, call somebody.

"Andrew LaMarche liked the way Bo handled this case," she mentioned.

"So?"

"So I'm going to call him."

Henry Benedict picked up a paperback history of the Civil War he'd been reading earlier. He knew his Latina wife. Impulsive, and she'd just reached the flash point. There would be no stopping her. So he didn't try.

Andrew LaMarche accepted the call, patched through from his service.

"*Bueno*," Estrella began excitedly, her accent deepening. "I'm Bo Bradley's friend. We share an office. I'm worried sick. I think something's wrong. I think Bo's tied up somehow in this case with the deaf boy and may get hurt."

Andrew LaMarche listened somberly. He knew about Angela Reavey, and felt a growing shame at his use of her name in yesterday's well-choreographed attack on Child Protective Services. The surgeon attending Reavey had phoned, at LaMarche's request, to say that the woman's condition was critical, but she had a chance.

And now this.

Bo Bradley was missing. LaMarche remembered the woman's deep excitement about the deaf boy. And her anger at his arrogance. He admired Bo Bradley. The thought of her coming to harm was painful.

"What do you want me to do?" he asked Estrella.

"I don't know," she answered, wound down now. "But there's got to be something."

"I'll think on it," LaMarche offered.

It was the least he could do.

24

Foster Care

Don't speed; stay with the traffic,'' Bo told the BMW as she joined the northbound traffic on Sunset Cliffs Boulevard. The landscape crawled beside her like a slow-motion travelogue. The San Diego River, flat as a mirror. Dog Beach on the left, where a man in a three-piece suit stood ankle-deep in sand, watching a long-haired dachshund sniff the cadaver of a small shark. Mildred loved Dog Beach. Bo hoped Estrella would take the little dog on outings there if something happened, and she couldn't do it herself.

The thought of Mildred alone brought tears to her eyes. She wanted to pull off the road and cry. Mildred had been a birthday gift from Mark, thirteen years ago. In another life, before a trucker hauling Vermont marble to a construction site in Poughkeepsie discovered Mary Laurie O'Reilly, dead beside the New York Thruway.

The little fox terrier was a link to a past Bo liked to remember. A time when she and Mark were going to work with native people. Bo had done a painting of a Navajo mother and child that UNICEF wanted to buy for their

Christmas card series. It would have launched a career in socially aware art. But then Laurie was dead and Bo couldn't stem the crashing tide of thoughts—the racing, crazy roller-coaster ride of ideas and feelings coming so fast she couldn't finish a sentence. Finally, she hadn't been able to talk at all and was hospitalized for three months. The only thing that hadn't changed when she came out was Mildred.

Far out to sea the marine layer hovered, a gray band of haze curving with the horizon. From its depths Bo thought she could hear the distant wail of Caillech Bera. The hag, haunting every windswept crossroad.

The image roused something deep within Bo.

"Aye, an' ye'll not be havin' me this time, Cally!" she yelled through trembling lips. "Ye'll have ta wait!"

Her grandmother's words. The familiar brogue. A source of strength when there was nothing else.

Bo wiped her tears on the sleeve of her sweatshirt and negotiated the complicated series of curving turns that would take her through the resorts fringing Mission Bay and into the old community of Pacific Beach. Minutes crept by with glacial stealth. Traffic. Out-of-season tourists with boogie-boards who'd turn blue after two minutes in the Pacific and then tell everyone back home they'd been surfing.

Finally. A right turn on Garnet, up a block, a left on Bayard—4917.

The house was a bungalow like all the others in the area. Wood frame, painted in gray and cream. A deck on the second story would provide a view of the sea. A child's bicycle with training wheels lay on its side in the grass. The Chandlers had children, or a child, of their own.

Bo parked the BMW across the Chandlers' driveway, but left the motor running.

What in hell now, Bradley?

Lights on. Cars in the drive. Everything looked normal. Dinnertime. They were probably eating. No squad cars, no Surf 'n' Sun rental cars. The men with guns hadn't arrived yet. But they would, and soon.

Bo rummaged under the seven-grain bread in her purse and found her ID badge. Clipping it to her sweatshirt, she hurried up the walk and knocked at the door. The man who answered sized her up in seconds, his eyes betraying that wariness Bo knew only too well.

Too late she remembered her uncombed hair, freshly washed and flying from her head in an electric tangle of silver-red curls. Bleary eyes from crying. No makeup. Dressed in sweats. Not a pretty picture.

Richard Chandler had seen what she was immediately. A crazy. Inappropriate. To be feared.

"Just came by to drop off a box of clothes," she mentioned casually. It was standard, when a child was placed in foster care. The social worker would bring the child's things from home, when possible, to save San Diego County the expense of providing wardrobes for thousands of kids every year. Except Weppo hadn't come from home. There were no clothes, no toys, no artifacts of a history.

Richard Chandler looked puzzled.

"What clothes?" he asked. "I don't see any clothes."

"In the car," Bo mumbled lamely. "Wanted to make sure I had the right address . . ."

You're blowing it, Bradley. Do something.

But what? The guy wasn't going to let her in the house. And anything she said would be written off as incomprehensible raving, even though Chandler would know about the attack on Weppo in the hospital. She wouldn't be able to speak slowly enough to be taken seriously, wouldn't be able to make sense.

"There's danger," Delilah Brasseur's words thrummed in the air. "So much danger it can't be told. Don't let nothin' happen to my baby..."

Bo glanced nervously at an immense jade plant beside the steps. Its fat, green leaves seemed ready to split from the pressure within them.

"Well?" Richard Chandler scowled.

And then a scream. A guttural, familiar, croaking scream as a little boy with huge tan eyes and hair like spun wire propelled himself past the man in the door and into Bo's arms.

"Weppo!" she breathed, hugging the small body tightly.

She wanted to cry, yell, sob, give expression to the tumult of emotion raging in her. And that would be the worst thing she could do.

"Let's go get your things out of the car," she chirped at the boy in her arms, casting what she hoped was a sweet smile over her shoulder at the balding man in khakis standing in the door. "Just a few things. We can carry them, can't we, tiger?"

All the back end workers called little boys "tiger." Bo hoped she sounded like one of them.

Richard Chandler had seen her badge. Didn't want to appear rude to the agency employing and paying him and his wife to care for foster children. Bo hoped the Chandlers were new at foster parenting—a pro would tackle her to the ground before permitting what she was about to do.

Pretending that the passenger's-side door was locked, Bo shrugged in mock exasperation and carried Weppo to the driver's side, and put him down. Predictably, he scrambled into the car as soon as she opened the door. Kids would do that. Especially a kid accustomed to confinement. Cars were a promise of movement, of something interesting to do.

Richard Chandler's scowl deepened as he started down the walk.

"Hey!"

No time left.

Bo flung herself into the car and jammed the gearshift into drive. The door slammed shut by itself when her foot hit the gas.

Get out of here!

Up to the corner of Bayard and Law. Right on Law three blocks to a street with no sign. Right again. Bo felt like a rat in a maze. Chandler would be after her. Maybe he'd call the cops first. As a licensed foster parent he would have been trained to do that. Surely he'd do that. But where should she go?

Weppo watched her, wide-eyed, from the passenger seat. Trusting. Interested.

"Don't let nothin' happen to my baby," a contralto voice whispered over the hum of the engine.

"Don't worry, Delilah Brasseur, whoever you are," Bo yelled aloud. "I've *got* your baby."

Quit yelling and go somewhere, Bradley.

But where? Interstate 5 was the main artery out of town. North, toward L.A., and south to Mexico. But that would be the first place the cops would look. Forget I-5.

Turning left on Grand, Bo followed the crowded street inland from the coast until it forked. The left fork was Balboa, which wended upward toward the residential community of Clairemont. Houses, apartments, condos, quiet shopping centers. The central bedroom community of San Diego. Nobody would expect her to flee there.

Weppo grinned and made the beer-drinking sign. The ride was a treat. He wanted a snack to celebrate.

At the corner of Balboa and Genesee Bo swerved into a gas station. If she were going somewhere, she'd have to have gas. Weppo jumped up and down on the front seat as she pumped, making his beer sign over and over.

It's dinnertime, Bradley. He's hungry. But who taught him that sign?

College kids favored it. Bo remembered the drug addict in a squash-colored car. "White male. Young. Maybe twenty-three," Bill Denny had said. The right age. Had he taught Weppo . . . ? Another memory intruded.

"I called the daddy to come get him, an' he did, but if somebody tried to kill the child out there, that mean the daddy already come to harm."

The daddy!

Bo shivered, paying for the gas. The young man dead of an overdose on a downtown street had been Weppo's father. But who was he? Why had the housekeeper for the Rowes called him to take Weppo away? Away from what?

Bo thought of warm coals beneath gray ash in a fireplace. A SpaghettiOs can. Weppo's father *had* meant to come back.

In the car the boy was growing impatient.

"Eat! Now!" the hand sign demanded.

"Your father is dead," Bo pronounced through tears.

Weppo rubbed his stomach under a navy blue T-shirt with "San Diego Padres" imprinted on it, and signed adamantly. Across the parking lot fronting a Mervyn's department store was a small Mexican restaurant. Bo eased the BMW behind it and parked.

"We'll eat," she smiled, cupping her right hand toward her mouth in the double movement that meant both eat and food in American Sign Language. Weppo copied the sign exactly, although Bo was sure he hadn't made the mental connection between the sign and the thing it represented. That would take time.

"And this," Bo pointed to the building, "is a restaurant.'' She made the crossed-fingers sign under her lips. Weppo duplicated it, studied the building's interior, looked at the cook dropping bent tacos into vats of hot oil, made the sign again.

Their chicken tacos would be ready in three minutes.

In the ladies' room Weppo attended to toileting with dispatch and then watched Bo attempt to make herself look less like the Madwoman of Chaillot. If the cops caught up with them, she wanted to look presentable for jail. As she shakily drew lipstick across her lips, the boy tugged on her shirt, pointed to his chin and drew his finger downward in a crook—the ASL sign for red.

The lipstick did little to create the illusion of calm, collected sanity she would need. She hadn't slept in two days. Even with the flesh-colored coverup stick, the skin around her eyes appeared greenish purple. Corpselike. Demented.

In the car she pulled apart another sedative and poured a little of its white powder into her Coke. She'd nurse it, drink it slowly on the way. The way to where?

Weppo, invigorated by his taco and orange juice, bounced on the front seat. There was no way to keep him still, keep him in his seat belt. And it was dangerous.

Overwhelmed, Bo eyed her drugged Coke and thought of offering the little boy a sip. No wonder somebody'd had him on Thorazine. He was all over the place.

But then Laurie had been that way too. It was still no excuse for drugging a child.

At a variety store in the shopping center Bo stopped again and took Weppo inside. Coloring books, paper, crayons, felt-tip pens, and a flashlight. It might work. From the trunk of her car she took the sleeping bag always kept there, and unrolled it across the backseat.

"There!" she signed, lifting him in. "You stay there."

Back on Balboa the streetlights were on, and the illuminated highway signs: "163 North," one indicated.

Where did that go? Bo tried to remember. Didn't it turn into 15? She'd been on 15 before, on her way...

That's it, Bradley.

Fifteen would take her out of town, into the desert. Fifteen was the way toward the Coso rock drawings, toward Owens Valley and Lone Pine. That's where she'd go. To the mystical figures painted on rock a thousand years ago. Bo could hear them sing to her. A chant of quiet, arid calm. And wasn't Annie Garcia in Lone Pine? For a pow-wow? Maybe Bo could find the old Indian woman somehow. Maybe Annie, and the rock drawings, would help her.

This is craziness, Bradley. Delusion. Do you know what you're doing?

Bo turned on the radio. Mozart. It would do.

Once she got somewhere, got Weppo to safety, she'd call Estrella. And if the police had captured the killers, she'd turn herself and Weppo in. But not until then.

In the dusk she saw the gleaming edge of a full moon rising.

Great. As if everything else weren't enough.

A full moon is not the friend of brains with strange chemistry. Bo knew the danger like a half-forgotten tune. The genesis, in fact, of the word "lunatic." She swallowed a sip of the Coke and sighed. There would be nothing poetic in this moon. Not for her. There would be nothing but danger.

25

"The Aginbite of Inwit ..."
—Gerard Manley Hopkins

The gas logs in the terra-cotta fireplace ignited with a whoosh when Andrew LaMarche flipped the switch concealed under one of the coffee table's hand-painted tiles.

The salty breeze from his balcony doors felt clammy. A tidy, ash-free fire, he hoped, would create a warmer atmosphere. The bachelor condo, furnished scrupulously to his specifications by a decorator brought down from Beverly Hills, seemed more and more like the interior of a glacier.

Over the hilly silhouette of Torrey Pines Reserve to the south, he could see the full moon rising against the bottomless black of a universe he rarely thought about. He had his work. There was no time for anything else.

The condo in the coastal San Diego suburb of Del Mar had been purchased less for its elite address than for its distance from St. Mary's Hospital. He would need to get away, he'd reasoned five years ago when he assumed the directorship of St. Mary's child abuse program. And he'd been correct.

But Torrey Pines became his home. The reserve, with its

scented paths through sandstone badlands, droves of wildflowers, and rare Torrey pines leaning over the sea, offered all the comfort he needed. A paradise of solitude, always there. The condo was only a place to sleep.

Except he couldn't sleep tonight. Something was gnawing at him. Something about the deaf boy, the unconscionable violence of the attack on the boy and the murder of Brad Sutin, a young orderly just trying to do his job. And something about the CPS investigator, Bo Bradley, who'd named him like an Irish bogy—a pompous boar, or was it "bore"? He felt like a bore. Gutless, in fact. Edgy, angry, watchful.

Accustomed to sporadic naps interrupted by grim emergencies, he'd stretched out on the bed an hour ago and found himself staring at the ceiling. Estrella Benedict's call hadn't wakened him. He'd been lost in thought. The soft roar of the gas jets in the fireplace seemed unable to create any semblance of warmth. The chill, he decided, was psychic, not physical. Might as well identify it. A chill left behind in New Orleans nearly a quarter century ago.

He hadn't thought about his daughter, her nameless grave in a parish paupers' field, in years. What was the point? Sylvie was dead. He devoted his life to other children, ones who might make it.

Sylvie hadn't made it. Sylvie was gone.

She'd been dead for two months before he came home to New Orleans on furlough from Vietnam and heard about her. His child's mother, the perennially exuberant Reena DuBois, hadn't been the one to tell him. Her brother, Joshua, had.

"Ree jus' couldn't take care of the baby," Josh wept in an alley behind a French Quarter bar where he played the same Scott Joplin ragtime tunes over and over for tourists.

"She lef' the baby alone, goin' out, partyin' . . . you know Ree . . ."

Alone one evening, the two-year-old had drowned in the deep, clawfoot bathtub of her mother's back-street apartment. She'd filled the tub, apparently, in an attempt to bathe her toys.

"Jus' like her daddy," Josh pronounced bitterly, sneering through tears at LaMarche's immaculate Marine Corps uniform. "She liked things *clean!*"

LaMarche had tried to find Ree for years, and failed. Throughout medical school and after, he'd hired tracers, private investigators. But for nothing. She'd left New Orleans the day after Sylvie's funeral. Vanished. Left no trace.

He stopped wondering if the child were really his at the moment Josh told him how she died. Sylvie was his. Reena DuBois hadn't named her baby after his mother out of spite. And his mother, dead seven years now, had never known about her granddaughter. Her black granddaughter, child of a beautiful young woman addicted to life, to fast times and bright lights.

LaMarche didn't blame Ree, he blamed himself. Ree had done the best she could with who she was. He had done nothing. His rage at every irresponsible parent whose child came through his program at St. Mary's was really at himself. He'd known that all along. Because he'd known all along that Sylvie's death was his fault.

He could have prevented it. Could have acknowledged paternity and provided money and care for the mocha-colored baby in the snapshots Ree sent to him in Da Nang. A pretty little girl, but she didn't look like him. Why had that mattered? She didn't look like Ree either. Just a baby. His family had plenty of money, but he hadn't wanted to embarrass them, bring down what his mother would have called disgrace. And Ree made no demands.

Theirs was a high school affair, begun when Ree was a dazzling cheerleader, the first black on the squad, and he was a second-string basketball player who might play in the fourth quarter if his team were twenty points in the lead, but even then only because everybody in New Orleans knew his social-climbing parents. They'd been friends more than lovers, he and Ree. Exploring the rituals of sex together as if researching a class project.

After he went away to college they got together occasionally on his visits home. Sex was a tradition between them by then. A way of bridging a widening gap.

Ree was wild, slept with anybody she wanted. He hadn't cared, until the phone call in his freshman year, when he'd already signed up with the marines. It had seemed the most expedient way to place a huge distance between himself and his parents. He'd been obsessed with getting away.

"I'm pregnant," she told him. "It's your baby."

"Mon Dieu!" was all he could say.

Pierre and Sylvie LaMarche, struggling desperately for acceptance in the historic reaches of New Orleans society, still spoke Cajun French at home. So did their son, Andrew, and his sister, Elizabeth. But the English names hadn't made a scratch on the truth about the LaMarches. Cajun commoners.

His parents were never listed in the social register.

Elizabeth, now a psychologist in Lafayette with a husband and three kids, one of whom had inherited his own fastidious nature, laughed long and frequently at the past.

"Our parents were just pathetic," she reminded him regularly. "Get a life, Andy! Come out of that noble, elegant shell and look around. Life's fun, but it's short, and you're not getting any younger. In case you hadn't noticed."

LaMarche strode into his kitchen and opened the refrigerator. It was so clean he could have performed surgery in the vegetable bin. And empty. He rarely ate at home.

But a single Waterford wine glass chilling in the freezer was the final straw. What was he doing, sitting around in Del Mar while madmen shot up hospitals, split open skulls of middle-aged women, tracked a deaf toddler as if he were the Antichrist, and might already have killed a moody Irishwoman who'd had the nerve to call his bluff?

Nothing. He was doing nothing.

Andrew LaMarche closed the refrigerator door softly and made a quiet decision.

It was time to rejoin the human race.

Pressed for an explanation he could not have said why it was time, but the challenge presented by a pair of flashing green eyes had been a catalyst. He could imagine Bo Bradley going to extreme lengths to protect this deaf boy she was so excited about. Alone, against professional assassins. She would do what she could in this bizarre scenario. And so, Andrew LaMarche decided in the unused gleam of his elegant kitchen, would he.

"This is Dr. LaMarche." He spoke with quiet authority to St. Mary's discharge clerk. "I'd like an update on a Johnny Doe who will have been discharged to a DSS foster home this afternoon."

The speaker of his state-of-the-art answering machine amplified the woman's sharp intake of breath.

"I'm sorry, but all information concerning that patient is flagged confidential," the voice informed him. "I have no way of knowing that you're really Dr. LaMarche. You may have the information, but only in person."

Irritating, but necessary under the circumstances, LaMarche conceded. Still, he wasn't about to drive all the way back into the city to get information on his own patient.

"I'm afraid I don't have time to come to the hospital in person. But Drs. Smith, Stracher, Dysinger, Cassavant,

Zollner, Koblenz, and Araldi are on duty. If you'll call one of them to the phone I'm sure we can confirm my identity.''

An extension was picked up. "Abe Zollner. That you, Andy? What's up?''

"Having a little trouble getting information on a patient DSS had flagged confidential—the boy that was shot at last night . . .''

"It's him,'' he heard Zollner tell the clerk.

"The boy was released to a confidential foster home at 3:30 this afternoon,'' she told LaMarche.

"The number is 489-6754. I'm sorry about the precautions.''

Nobody answered the phone at the foster home. LaMarche hung up and dialed again, in case he'd made a mistake. Two rings. Four. Five. Finally a breathless male voice answered.

"Hello. Who is this?''

"Dr. LaMarche, from St. Mary's Hospital—''

"How did you find out so fast?'' the man gasped. "It just happened. Twenty minutes ago. The police just got here . . . Oh, my God, Timmy, thank God . . .''

The man was upset, nearly hysterical. In the background LaMarche could hear a woman crying, hiccupping, trying to talk. "What's happened?'' he asked slowly.

"They came here,'' the man exploded. "The guys with the guns, right after that crazy Bradley woman took the deaf boy. I tried to stop her. But she just grabbed him and beat all hell out of here, and then I called the cops and before they got here those guys, those fucking shitbags . . .''

"Was anyone hurt?'' LaMarche asked softly.

"No, thank God, not bad. They threw Caroline against a wall, and one of them held a gun to my head, but they thought our son, Timmy, was the deaf kid and if he hadn't yelled 'Mommy' they'd have shot him . . .''

The man was sobbing.

"I'll check in later,'' LaMarche said, and hung up.

Estrella Benedict answered on the first ring.

"Bo has apparently kidnapped the boy from the foster home," LaMarche told her quietly. "Got him out only minutes before the killers arrived. The foster father described her as crazy. Where would she go? Do you have any idea?"

"*Madre de dios!*" Estrella choked. "Bo got the kid! She saved his life!"

LaMarche sensed that Estrella was conveying the information to someone else, probably her husband.

"But now she's in grave danger," he prompted. "Where would she go?"

"She wouldn't go to her apartment. Surely she wouldn't. They'd go there first, wouldn't they?"

"Yes," LaMarche agreed grimly.

"But it's all we've got, right?" Estrella was in gear. "Meet us there. My husband, Henry, has a gun. Bo's place is the last apartment building on Narragansett, on the left, off Sunset Cliffs Boulevard in Ocean Beach."

"I'm leaving now," LaMarche said.

It was the first time in two decades that he'd gone out without socks. But he didn't notice.

26

Not Quite Alone in the Dark

Weppo clambered, chimplike, between the back and front seats several thousand times by Bo's estimation before 163 became 15 as she had begun to doubt it would. The highway looked alien, unfamiliar.

With each bounce into the front seat, Weppo tugged at her sleeve and held up yet another crayon or marker. He wanted to know the signs for colors, and Bo had successfully shown each one, stumped only by cerulean blue and now magenta.

Was there a sign for magenta? She couldn't remember. Years of signing with Laurie, and she'd forgotten magenta. In the dim glow of the dash lights she saw the little boy regard the crayon seriously and then flip his first and second fingers from his chin toward his chest. The ASL sign she'd taught him for pink. He'd figured it out by himself. It was a miracle, illuminated as if by candlelight in the dark capsule of the car.

The lines were blurring, Bo realized. She wasn't sure who was saving whom, or from what. The wiry-haired, pale child might be an angel. The light in his eyes propelling them to unknown destinations. To safety. An angel signing colors in a nicotine-smelling BMW that had seen better days. Bo wondered if angels could sign, imagined the heavenly host signing the Christmas scriptural message generally attributed to them across Bethlehem's black sky. Their hands would sparkle and flash like a light show. Like Weppo's hands. The image made her grin. And then frown.

Rational, concrete thought was more difficult in the dark. Tenuous. Quixotic. Her mind wanted to, would, create fanciful pictures instead. And her feelings would reflect the pictures, not reality. Or else it was the other way around, and the feelings created the mind-pictures. Either way, it was the last stage before the dissolution, the meltdown of ten million fine wires connecting her to the world everyone else experienced. And that couldn't happen! Not now.

The ice in the druggy Coke had melted. She sloshed the weak solution around in its container and took another deep drink. The sedative wouldn't really help the kaleidoscoping images, the torrents of feeling. Only the lithium would do that, and not until it permeated her bloodstream. Weeks.

Weppo scooted into the backseat again and aimed his flashlight on a sheet of paper. "Blue," he signed, and carefully slid all the blue crayons from the box.

"I love you," Bo told the child's reflection in the rear-view mirror. "I want you to have a life."

Damn the lithium and its patient, practical progress! She needed it now. And what was it, anyway? A natural element, leached from stone. 7-Up, she'd heard, put it in their drink in the days before the Food and Drug Administration monitored such things. A stone drink. Was it for statues?

Bo wanted to be stone, wanted the stuff like an armature in her body. She thought of rocks, of their different experiences of time. Whole lifetimes could pass, wars fought, won, and lost, while a rock just sat there, slowly crumbling.

No wonder it took lithium so damn long. It was stone, with a stone's sense of urgency. Which was no urgency at all.

Weppo handed a picture of a taco across the seat. A blue taco, surprisingly recognizable.

"Blue food," he signed, standing up so she could see over her shoulder.

"Yes," she signed with her fist. "Blue Food."

He was so bright, and obviously gifted. A taco, Bo realized, was one hell of a thing to draw. The depth was the problem, the curve of a flat object on a two-dimensional surface made to appear three-dimensional. And he'd done it. How? Who had taught him to draw but not taught him to talk?

Nobody, she realized. He was just a natural.

All the more reason to keep your shit together, Bradley. This kid may turn out to be the twenty-first century's answer to Renoir. Keep him alive.

Bo grabbed a slice of the abominable seven-grain bread from her purse and bit off a piece. It would buffer the sedative.

Weppo yawned and lay down on the sleeping bag, signing colors at his crayons with pale, short fingers.

Ahead lay the immigration checkpoint at the border between San Diego County and Riverside County. Empty. Nobody was checking for illegal aliens tonight, and Bo drove under the white, barred signs like a fugitive. She'd forgotten about immigration. Thank God they weren't there.

Signs to Indio and to Hemet flashed past, then the 215 turnoff. Was that the way she'd gone before? It felt right. Something in the bread cleared her head momentarily, she guessed.

The headlights of a car behind her veered to the right of 215 as she did. Odd. The lights, she realized as a wad of bread stopped halfway down her throat, had kept that same distance behind her for miles.

27

A Map in the Moon

Andrew LaMarche had no trouble identifying Bo's apartment. It was the only one of four in the building whose door gaped open, revealing overturned furniture, broken lamps, books, and papers heaped on the floor.

A sixth sense told him no one was there, but he entered cautiously nonetheless. The killers had known where to find Bo. They'd gone to her apartment after their failed attempt on the child's life and left the picture of a decapitated dog as a warning of what they would do if she meddled further. Bo had been furious when she arrived at the hospital last night, her little dog tucked inside her blazer. The dog was safe now with Estrella, but the danger to Bo was a thousand times greater. LaMarche jammed his fists into jeans pockets and wondered if Bo Bradley was as scared right now as he was.

"Hay-soos!" yelped a voice behind him as Estrella and Henry Benedict breathlessly mounted the stairs. "They've been here!"

"Oui," LaMarche replied nervously. "Estrella, you know Bo. Where would she have gone?"

Henry Benedict closed the door, locked it, introduced himself and began prowling through the apartment. LaMarche noted with comfort the black .45 caliber service automatic in the man's right hand.

"I wish I could tell you something." Estrella sighed. "But Bo stayed here most of the time when she wasn't at work. The job," she told LaMarche pointedly, "doesn't leave much time for a wild social life. We work weekends. It's never done . . ."

LaMarche acknowledged the chastisement with a polite nod. "But now, with the deaf boy, where would she run?"

Estrella regarded him closely, her mascaraed black eyes searching his face, his sweater and Levi's, his bare ankles and loafers as if for a clue to something. She seemed unsure.

"What is it?" he asked.

She tossed her black hair and looked him in the eye. A decision. Made.

"There's something you don't know about Bo," she explained. "It's hard to know where she's gone, because, well . . . Bo's different. I mean her mind works . . . different."

LaMarche was puzzled.

Under a purple cashmere sweater Estrella's shoulders squared above a deep breath.

"Bo's a manic-depressive," she stated finally. "Nobody knows except me, and Henry. She'd lose her job. You can't tell anybody."

"Mon Dieu!" LaMarche breathed. He knew little about the major mental disorders. One course years ago in medical school. He was a pediatrician, not a psychiatrist.

"Lithium." The word rose into consciousness from some long-forgotten textbook.

"She takes the lithium when she has to," Estrella explained. "When it starts to get bad. She knows what to do. She's taking it now, but she just started and it takes..."

"Three weeks. About three weeks," LaMarche finished the phrase. It was coming back, the minuscule information he'd memorized for an exam, and then forgotten. *How* had she managed to rescue the boy, under those circumstances?

Henry Benedict had phoned the police.

"A patrol car'll be here in five or ten minutes," he told them. "They'll take a report. But there won't be a detective on this case until Monday."

LaMarche made a dive for the phone. He knew a dozen good psychiatrists in San Diego, but there was somebody better.

"Elizabeth?"

His sister was, fortunately, at home.

"This is Andy. I don't have time to explain. It's an emergency. Just give me an idea of what a manic-depressive might do, running from a life-threatening situation."

"In a manic or a depressive episode?" she asked quickly.

He remembered green eyes, clear and intense, flashing at him in anger only yesterday. Bo had shown none of the telltale signs of depression, only an abundance of affect.

"Manic," he decided.

Estrella confirmed it.

"Bo gets manic, mostly. She told me it only went the other way once, after her sister committed suicide. She had to... you know... go in a hospital. She said the depression's the worst, like a poison that doesn't have the decency to kill you."

LaMarche was sure Bo had said precisely that. The gift for drama, the creative flair.

"Your manic will do what anybody else would do, only in an exaggerated way," Elizabeth explained. "Look for the person's—is this a man or a woman?—symbol system. What do they care about? What's important to them? What belief system keeps them going? You know . . . like a manicky priest might run to the church where he was ordained, or a nature lover might run to a favorite spot in the woods . . .''

LaMarche handed the phone to Estrella.

"You know the answers," he urged her. "Talk to my sister. She's a psychologist. See if you can figure out where Bo's gone."

LaMarche poked randomly though the ravaged apartment. He had no idea what he was looking for. Beside an overturned easel was an unfinished painting. A bighorn sheep, rendered in primitive, stick-figure form. Around the sheep were smaller figures—spirals, mandalas, humanlike images with rectangular bodies and heads that looked like targets wearing round earrings. All the figures appeared to be emerging from a pile of rocks. Or caught in a pile of rocks. LaMarche couldn't tell which.

The painting's source of light was the moon. A full moon, on which close inspection revealed more of the figures, hundreds of them buried in the shine of gray-white paint. Were the moon-figures calling the rock-figures to life, or merely reflections of them? He stared dizzily into the painting thrown atop Black Watch plaid sheets on the bed. The answer to where Bo Bradley would go, he realized, lay in the picture. But it might as well have been a blank canvas.

"Bo doesn't exactly have a belief system, like your sister said," Estrella explained, approaching the painting. "She's not, you know, religious or anything. She likes to tell these Irish stories, folk tales or something. And lately this has been her main thing, these Indian paintings."

"What Indians?" LaMarche asked. "Where did she learn about these figures?"

"She goes out in the desert someplace," Estrella answered. "She told me where, but—"

"Look at this," Henry mentioned, holding up a book he'd found under the bed. "It's about Paiute Indians in Owens Valley up around Lone Pine. Pictures of these rock-drawings. Some of the pages are torn out."

"Lone Pine! That's it! Bo's been up there," Estrella cried.

LaMarche scanned the book.

"There's something else," Estrella thought aloud. "Bo told me the old Indian woman who found the little boy and then remembered the license number was going up there today—to Lone Pine. Your sister said Bo would try to get to somebody she trusts, somebody that seems like a part of the symbol system."

The figures in the painting. The interest in folklore. It all came together for LaMarche: Bo was fleeing with the boy to the Indians in Lone Pine, to one Indian who'd already saved the child's life. An old woman, a powerful symbol in the Celtic tales she'd undoubtedly heard as a child. It made sense.

He glanced at his watch. Bo had been gone for almost two hours. He could never catch up with her. Not in a car...

"Listen to this," Henry yelled from the living room.

"My name is Delilah Brasseur," a black voice in the patois of the deep South filled the room as Henry upped the volume. "Until two weeks ago I was the housekeeper for the Rowes..."

When the message was over they stared at the machine.

"Who in hell are the Rowes?" Henry blurted.

"Bo's on to more than we knew," LaMarche decided. "Make sure the police bag that tape for the detectives. Stay here until they get here. I'm going after Bo."

"How?" Henry and Estrella asked as one.

There was a way. And a man who would help. The man who'd covered for LaMarche in Vietnam after Sylvie died. The man who'd taken his shifts in surgery and lied to the C.O. and finally carried him bodily out of a Saigon brothel where Andrew Jacques LaMarche, AWOL and drunk for two weeks straight, hadn't cared which came first—death or dishonorable discharge. And Rudy Palachek would, LaMarche was sure, be more than happy to help find men who shot mercury-tipped bullets at sleeping children.

"That friend of yours at Pendleton," he asked Palachek on the phone, "the copter pilot. Can he liberate a chopper and get us off the roof at the hospital in forty-five minutes?"

Five minutes later Palachek called back. "Affirmative. He'll be at the copter pad in half an hour. And Andy... ?" Rudy Palachek's tone was firm. "I get the kill."

28

Joshua Trees

The car, like a reversed image of her own headlights, continued to follow. Always at a precise distance, as if she were towing it.

Two hours ago at 9:30 P.M., skirting the city of Riverside, Bo had made a final decision. There would be no pulling off, going to police, relinquishing Weppo to yet another system identical to San Diego's, which would not be able to protect him. The Riverside Police, dazzled by her warp-speed speech and bizarre story, would undoubtedly have taken her politely and swiftly to their county's psychiatric facility. There, a perfectly legal seventy-two-hour observation hold would have confined her behind locked doors with a well-meaning staff who'd listen absently to her story, and then say, "Try to rest now." Weppo would have gone to a receiving home and on Monday another investigator, another foster home. Except that by Monday, Weppo would be dead.

Besides, she'd tried to think rationally, maybe the car wasn't following, but just one of those cautious night

146

drivers who like to stay behind somebody else's taillights. Not surprisingly, the rational approach had proven to be a comforting illusion, bearing no relation to fact.

Somebody was following her. Speeding and slowing as she did. Staying just far enough back that she couldn't identify the make of the car or see the license plates.

But why? The desert road was sparsely traveled. They could overtake her anywhere, force her off the road, shoot her and Weppo, and then just vanish. Nobody would see them. Nobody was there.

Or was there? In the eerie, moonlit landscape of the high desert Bo was aware of distorted forms. Armies of the twisted, multi-armed Joshua trees the Mormons named "devil trees" for their grotesque appearance. A desert growth that made people nervous. The Joshua tree, Bo felt, was kin.

She could see them, tearing loose shallow roots and walking toward the killers. A hundred Joshua trees moving scratchily across the desert floor and wrapping two men in a thousand black, cactusy arms. Mercury bullets wouldn't harm them. They'd keep coming. They'd lacerate, crush the murderous human flesh in the car behind her. There would be nothing left but mutilated pulp clinging to two skeletons. And two useless guns.

"Stay with me," she called to them with her mind as the car ate mile after mile of desert road. "I may need you." The strange trees, one after another, seemed to bow in acknowledgment. As if they'd known for centuries this would happen, and were ready.

Weppo had crawled inside the sleeping bag and fallen asleep. Bo could see tufts of his hair blowing in the breeze from her open window. Angel hair. Burnished gold wire. The stuff of which a bridle might be woven to fit a unicorn. Or a torque for a daughter of Lir.

Bo remembered the children of the ancient king—children

turned to swans and doomed to fly forever in rains of ice over black and storm-tormented winter lakes, until the day when the mountains would open again, and the lost faerie kingdoms would be restored to the world.

"Aye, an' ye're one," her grandmother had crooned sadly. "Ye an' wee Laurie too. Ye're like swans, the children of Lir."

Bo felt like a swan, soaring low over a lake bottom frozen in arid silence. Ahead the Paso Mountains might hold deep within their prehistoric hugeness some faerie kingdom, some kind and splendid race of beings whose mirth and poetry would restore balance to a world gone mad with greed.

At the turnoff for the China Lake Naval Weapons Center— the once-sacred land of a vanished people who'd left symbol-tapestries painted on rock—Bo felt the car stall and catch again. A cough in the engine. A hiccup.

You're out of gas, idiot! This is what they were waiting for.

A glance at the fuel gauge confirmed it. Empty.

Your stupidity is monstrous. You are crazy. Because of you, they're going to kill him.

The car coughed and stalled again. Slowed. Died.

Through wild tears Bo eased if off the road and appealed one last time to the weird trees and the forgotten figures painted on canyon walls thousands of years ago.

"Now!" she begged them as the car behind slowed, and stopped.

A falling star high above left a brief arc, but nothing else moved. Bo leaped over the seat and flung herself on the boy in the sleeping bag as footsteps approached on the gravelly shoulder of the road. Inside the blood roar in her ears Bo heard the laughter of Caillech Bera.

A chuckle, actually.

Words.

"You must be Bo Bradley," a woman's voice said cheerily. "I've been following you for hours. Sorry if I scared you, but you never stopped for gas, and I didn't want to lose you . . ."

Wakened by 125 pounds of frantic weight on top of him, Weppo croaked peevishly and blinked at Bo, then the stranger.

A slightly overweight woman with close-cropped reddish blonde hair. Sparking blue eyes. Jeans and a sweaty T-shirt imprinted with the sentence "I Don't Have to Go to Hell When I Die; I've Been to Houston!" The woman looked like neither a Joshua tree nor a rock-drawing.

"I'm Bo Bradley, all right," Bo gasped, "but who are you?"

"Gretchen Tally. *Bayou Banner.* You called me in Houston, left a message about somebody trying to murder a Rowe child. My editor's desperate to stop Tia Rowe from winning that senate seat. That's desperate with a capital D and that rhymes with C and that stands for corrupt, if you know what I mean. You're our last hope for keeping her out of power. The paper flew me here with its last dime and instructions to use *anything.* So what've you got? The only Rowe kid left around is Kep. Where is he?"

"Who's Kep?" Bo asked thickly. The sedative had taken its toll on her ability to speak. The words felt like dustballs stuck to her tongue as she climbed out of the car into chill desert air. Weppo stumbled out as well, and sleepily went behind the car to relieve himself. Tally checked Bo out, and frowned.

"Is something the matter with you?" she questioned bluntly.

"Nothing that rebirth as a gnome in another galaxy won't cure," Bo answered. "Look, I'm as mad as a hatter, manic.

Off the wall. I'm serious. I really am a manic-depressive, and this is not, as they say, one of my better days. But you've got to believe me, somebody's trying to kill this kid. You've got to help us. My car's out of gas. I thought you were the killers. We have to get to Lone Pine. Delilah Brasseur said it'd be over by Tuesday—''

"Slow down, slow down," Gretchen Tally admonished. "I believe you. I want to help you and the kid, so talk slow. You mentioned Deely Brasseur; she was the Rowes' housekeeper. If there's anything fishy in that house, she's the only one who'd know. What did she tell you?"

Weppo came around the car, shivering and giggling while signing, "Food! Blue food, yellow food, pink food, purple food . . ."

Bo grabbed her purse and the seven-grain bread off the front seat and signed bread for Weppo.

"Brown," he signed back, and nibbled unenthusiastically on a slice.

"He's deaf," Bo told Gretchen Tally. "Nobody's ever taught him to sign. Until now."

"Let's get in my car and get going," the reporter suggested. "You'll explain all this to me as we go. Meanwhile, I want you to see something . . ."

With Tally's help Bo moved the sleeping bag and Weppo's toys to the other car and then locked her own. She wondered if she'd ever see it again, or if it would be appropriated by the Joshua trees for trips to wherever Joshua trees went.

"Look," the other woman indicated, handing Bo a Houston newspaper. On its front page was a photo of Tia Rowe in black, her eyes concealed behind a veil. The headline read, "Shipping Heir MacLaren Rowe Succumbs to Heart Attack." The article beneath the picture promised that the widow, despite an untimely burden of grief, would carry on the tradition of the Rowe name by remaining in the closely contested state senate race to be decided on Tuesday, also the day for which MacLaren Rowe's funeral had been scheduled.

"She's won the damn thing." Tally grimaced, pulling onto the road. "She'll slide in on the sympathy vote. Unless you've got something to tell me that'll make a difference. Now, for starters, what did the Brasseur woman tell you, who's this deaf kid, and where's Kep Rowe?"

Bo took a deep breath.

"This deaf kid is Weppo. He was nearly murdered last night in a hospital room by one of two men and a mercury-tipped hollow-point bullet shot from a silenced Smith & Wesson .38," Bo recited as one long word. "I've never heard of Kep Rowe. I assume he has something to do with Tia Rowe, Houston's answer to toxic waste. The lady with rattlesnake eyes. The one person who might actually find employment decorating rest rooms for third world bus stations. The—"

"All right!" Gretchen Tally laughed. "God, I wish I had a tape recorder. Can you slow down at all?"

"Probably not," Bo replied. She trusted Gretchen Tally completely, the manicky radar full-blown now, picking up nothing but competence and solid intelligence in the chunky woman. But the release from responsibility Tally provided wasn't helping Bo's grip on reality. "I'm really going off," she told the reporter. "I'm going to take part of another sedative, but it'll probably knock me out for a while. Just get us to Lone Pine. We've got to find a woman named Annie Garcia. She's a Paiute. She's the one who found Weppo tied to a mattress up on the reservation . . ."

Bo found the capsules in her purse and again poured more than half out of one into the car's ashtray.

"Here's a Coke to knock that back with." Tally offered a can from a small cooler between the seats. "But stay awake long enough to tell me why Weppo has anything to do with Tia Rowe. Kep Rowe is the son, incidentally.''

''I found a grocery receipt from Jamail's,'' Bo began after swallowing the capsule, ''near where a car that we later found out was stolen in Houston and a wino found a dead drug addict in was parked . . .''

The words didn't sound right, the syntax all wrong.

''I'm not making any sense, am I?'' she asked Gretchen Tally.

''Enough. Go on before you're out cold.''

''After they shot at Weppo, the cops told me nobody'd investigate until next week, and I knew there wasn't time, so I flew to Houston and found out the receipt was the Rowes', and the maid wouldn't let me in, but there was this picture, this old photograph on the wall—appalling wall paper—of a little boy, late 1800s, early 1900s—and it looks just like Weppo! I mean, they're identical. And—''

''That's probably the famous Wilhelm Marievski, Tia's father,'' Gretchen interjected. ''The Polish artist. An abstractionist. Had his own 'school' in Chicago. His paintings are worth a fortune now. Tia—her real name's Skiltia—was the only child.''

Bo could feel the drug dragging her into sleep, but she fought it. ''Wilhelm.'' Something about the name . . . She forced her mouth to pronounce it slowly, and then watched herself in the car's exterior side mirror. There it was! Lipreading her own mouth, she saw the syllables— ''We-eh-po!''

''That's Weppo's name!'' she told Tally. ''His name's Wilhelm!''

''I still don't know of a connection to Tia. She and that pathetic lush of a husband only had two kids—Kep and Julie. Julie died, about four years ago. I wasn't around then. I was still in school—journalism, Indiana University—but I dug out the old clips. Supposedly it was a brain tumor. But there's something fishy about that story. And Kep's a chip off the old block, except his thing's drugs instead of booze. Hey, didn't you say something about a dead drug addict?''

Bo could not stay awake any longer.

"The dead druggie was Weppo's father. I'm sure of it," she managed to pronounce. "The killers are still after Weppo. Danger . . . just get us to Lone Pine . . . find Annie . . . if anything happens . . . Joshua trees . . .'' Bo was gone, slumped on the seat like a damp envelope.

"We'll get there," Gretchen Tally reassured herself more than Bo Bradley. She needed to get to a phone. If this deaf boy was Kep Rowe's son . . . She shivered and turned on the car's heater. The story taking shape in her mind was too much for a green cub reporter. She had to call her editor. But it couldn't be . . . It was impossible. Nobody could be that vile. Nobody.

29

The Candidate

A palmetto bug, oily black as the prehistoric sludge in which its ancestors had frolicked, skittered across Paris-yellow rosebud wallpaper and came to rest just below an ornately framed watercolor of willow trees under a Roman bridge. The bug waved inch-long glassine feelers in the direction of a woman seated at a dressing table, plucking already perfectly arched eyebrows.

Tia Rowe ignored the bug as she had ignored countless others before it. The oversized roaches were part of every domestic landscape in Houston. People learned to live with them. And Tia Rowe could live with *anything*, provided there was something in it for her. That was obvious. Hadn't she lived for twenty-five years with the drunken joke of a man whose funeral arrangements she had just completed?

The funeral director, dripping solicitousness, had pointed out several times too many that an election day memorial service might be considered "inappropriate" by many of the "fine, old families" expected to attend. Tia had hunched further beneath a stifling black cape donned for the occasion, and sniffled into a lace handkerchief. Something about travel arrangements, out-of-town relatives, a dear cousin—Mac's best friend, really, who couldn't possibly make connections from Barbados on such short notice, if at all. He'd need to be one of the pallbearers, of course. Unless he really couldn't make it. And who did the funeral director suggest as a stand-in?

She'd managed to appear grief-stricken, a little flighty, but determined. Precisely the image she wanted. The director had capitulated, even to the viewing to be held from 3:00 to 6:00 Monday afternoon.

The day before the election, Tia Rowe would stand beside her husband's mahogany casket and solemnly receive the condolences of Houston's society. From time to time she'd courteously step outside with a dignitary—the mayor, a state representative, a bishop, and converse in muted tones.

She'd already notified photographers from both major papers exactly where to stand in order to capture these moments for the evening editions. Every voter in Harris County who could read a newspaper Monday night would go to the polls on Tuesday impressed with the image of Tia Rowe as an aristocrat, one tough lady, who could keep it together when the going got rough.

In his lifetime Mac Rowe had not done her a greater kindness than dying three days before the election.

She whipped a silver-and-ebony brush through her hair and then carefully smoothed beeswax facial cream around her eyes. Too bad she couldn't have known Mac would choose this particular day to die exactly as the doctor had warned seven months ago.

"Your husband will be dead from massive internal hemorrhaging within the year," Foster Rhynders had told her quietly after a dinner party at the club, "unless he stops drinking."

She wished she'd known it would be today. She wouldn't have panicked about losing the election. Wouldn't have been in such a rush for the money to pay off some of the astronomical campaign expenses and secure credit for the eleventh-hour media blitz her staff told her she needed to defeat that tedious hausfrau Yannick.

But everything was under control now. Except for the messy business in California. And that would be finished tonight, they'd told her. For what she was paying them, it had better.

Tia Rowe gazed at the immense insect on her wall and thought about Deely Brasseur. The housekeeper she'd only kept on because *somebody* had to clean up after Mac and his disgusting, drunken messes. Tia wasn't about to do it, and neither would anybody else she could hire. Deely did it so she could spend half her life up in the attic fawning over Julie's brat, an imbecile that should have been aborted. *Would* be aborted, now.

She wondered how Deely had figured it out, when Tia had told her the Rowes would no longer require her services. Had Deely seen the bags of quicklime stacked in the garage? What would that mean to an ignorant old black maid? No, Deely couldn't have known the purpose for which Tia Rowe needed sixty pounds of calcium oxide. No one had known.

And it would have been so easy, once Deely was gone. A simple overdose of the Thorazine Tia used to keep the boy quiet up there. She flew down to Brownsville every few months and then slipped over the Mexican border into Matamoros where she could buy the drug over the counter. No questions. Untraceable. *So* easy. And the body could have stayed in the attic until Mac finally died and Tia could move on. The quicklime would have eaten away the four-year-old's remains in less than a week. That had been the plan. Until some stupid, shuffling servant caught on, and got Kep involved, and then ran off to hide. Deely would have to be silenced. But that could wait.

Nobody, Tia was certain, would believe Deely Brasseur, even if she told what she knew.

"A child in my attic?" Tia would frown and then murmur, "You know, we had to let Deely go, poor thing, right before Mac's death. She's, well . . . not right in the head, you know? But of course, I want y'all to feel free to look in the attic, if you want . . ."

Kep had been no problem, until Deely dragged him into the nonsense about the child. A drug addict, out of his mind most of the time. As his mother, Tia could have had him committed and assumed guardianship over the fortune he would inherit at twenty-three, anytime. She hadn't really intended for Kep to die, at least not at first. Only the idiot child her daughter had perished giving birth to. A retarded monster whose pointless existence could ruin everything.

Selecting a comfortable gown from her closet, Tia switched off the phone and slipped easily between creamy satin sheets. There would be no more coded messages tonight. And tomorrow it would all be over.

She wondered how long it would be before somebody identified the body now tagged in a San Diego morgue as her son's. Maybe they never would. It scarcely mattered. What mattered was to look good for the show of stalwart grief she would stage tomorrow. And for that she needed a good night's sleep.

30

Bureaucracy

I'm afraid there will be no choice but to terminate Bo's employment with the department," Madge Aldenhoven told Estrella Benedict with finality. "I know she may have saved the boy's life at the foster home, but this melodramatic behavior sets a precedent others will feel obliged to imitate. Bo isn't the only worker with an endangered child on her caseload, you know. All these children are in danger, or we wouldn't be dealing with them in the first place. I'm sure you can see—"

"I don't believe you!" Estrella screamed into her kitchen phone while Henry paced behind her. "I called to tell you what's happening and you tell me you're going to fire Bo! She's out there someplace right now, risking her life to keep this kid alive, and you—" Estrella couldn't go on.

"She's out there behaving like some damned *hero* in spite of my clear directions to stay off this case," Aldenhoven continued angrily. "There's more to consider here than just one child. There are over six hundred workers in this system, and every one of them is involved with children

158

who may get killed! The primary rule is never to get emotionally entangled in a case. And we all know Bo has trouble maintaining appropriate emotional responses..."

"What you're saying is," Estrella said, seething, "that the system comes before the children. That Bo should have let this kid get killed rather than violate the rule. Is that right?"

"If you want to put it that way," Madge replied shakily. "You know I actually like Bo personally, but—"

"But you're going to fire her for trying to save a kid's life? That is, if she isn't already dead? You're *loca*, Madge! You've been in the system so long you think it's a fucking religion, but it's not. It's just a fucking rotten job. And Bo is a hero! She's—"

"She's incapable of following instructions, and that's what counts, in this fucking rotten job!" Aldenhoven screamed back, out of control. "My decision is final."

"You don't even care if Bo gets killed," Estrella sobbed. But Aldenhoven had hung up.

31

White Flower Twining Down

A chill, shadowy wind blew the smell of snow down from the Sierra and through a chink in the window of a small room where Annie Garcia lay on her great-granddaughter's bed. She didn't sleep, but merely waited. Something was coming up out of the desert, from Coso where the Ancient Ones painted magic on the canyon walls, from Bitter Lake where the Paiute lost at last the hopeless battle for this strange, arid land.

The girl slept with friends in a tent outside—a re-creation of the woven-twig dwelling Annie's grandmother had slept beneath in a spring long ago, and named herself White Flower for the twining clematis. In the old times girls took flower names for the ritual of entry into womanhood, and Charlie encouraged his daughter to do so. "Paintbrush, then," the girl had chosen for the red-orange desert plant she loved. And she'd dutifully stacked piles of wood outside the tent five times a day. Piles of wood measured to her own height, as tradition demanded. Nobody had done such a ritual since before Annie's birth, but Charlie had gotten books from the library. This was what the books said Paiute girls did. Annie could see sense in it—the lifting and stretching would help diminish menstrual cramps.

Annie laughed with the snow-wind in the little room. The wind from a place where her grandmother had lived. Charlie wanted the old way, but not entirely. Not the young men in eagle feathers squatting silently at the foot of his daughter's blankets, asking for her hand in marriage, now that she was a woman. Charlie had skipped that part. Not that it would make any difference. Life was life, and would have its way. In the snow-wind Annie felt the breath of her grandmother twining down, joining her laughter, stretching further into the future through the young girl outside who would be called Paintbrush. It was good, whatever it meant.

But the thing in the desert, that wasn't good. Something terrifying, complex. Like a woven basket unraveling. The need to remember the pattern, mend the break even as it tore loose. Impossible.

Annie had been named Sees the Dark as a child, high in the snow-wind. She saw now, and was ready.

32

Lone Pine

Bo woke from a dream in which her back was breaking beneath the weight of an entire mountain range. Straightening, she realized she'd passed out bent over double, her head pressed against the dash. The resultant pounding ache between her temples reminded her of continents breaking apart, earthquakes, tidal waves. And where in hell was she?

From Gretchen Tally's car, parked in the gravel surrounding a vacant gas station, she saw what appeared to be a scrubby ghost town. Lightless houses. Shapes of darkened cars hunched on a grayly backlit street. A movie set. If she got out of the car, the forms would be revealed as cardboard cutouts. A fake town, shimmering hollowly under the huge blind eye of the moon. In the backseat a frizzy halo of hair erupted from a sleeping bag she recognized as her own. Weppo!

He's here. It's okay. Stop imagining things. Get it together.

In a phone booth that seemed real enough, Bo could see Gretchen Tally poring through a pencil-thin directory while holding an elf-sized flashlight in her teeth. Her face, illuminated from the nose up, looked like a nursery rhyme moon.

"Hey, diddle, diddle . . ." Bo hummed.

That won't do, Bradley. Clean it up.

But it wouldn't clean up. Images, distortions, strangeness loomed at Bo from all sides. Things being both what they were and what they meant, or might mean. Distilled and tangential at the same time. Gretchen Tally in the phone booth now a laughing manikin fortune-teller at a carnival. Eerie and portentous. A child's nightmare.

Shit! Eat something! Take something! Do something! This isn't going to cut it. You can't get crazy—not yet!

"I found a Charlie Garcia in the phone book," Gretchen Tally yelled as Bo sprang out of the car and sprinted around it. "Why are you running around the car?"

"Clears my head," Bo gasped. The air was like ice water in her lungs, against her skin. Probably a good idea. In the old days, she remembered from some textbook, they threw psychotic patients into icy lakes. Those that didn't die from shock and exposure often benefited from the experience. At least that was the theory. Bo flapped her arms and ran faster.

"And I called my editor," Tally went on. "I need to get a few answers from you, and then call him back. He's doing some research in the meantime. Get back in the car, Bo. You're going to get pneumonia out here."

Bo crawled inside, shivering. "What questions?"

"How do you know Delilah Brasseur, and what did she tell you?"

Bo reached over to the backseat and smoothed Weppo's hair. Clenched in his fist was a red felt-tip pen.

"I don't know her," Bo said with a sigh. "She left a message for me. She said I should take Weppo, 'the baby' is what she said, and go someplace where nobody could find us until Tuesday. She said it would be over Tuesday."

Comparisons to angel-messages promoting flights into Egypt were unavoidable. Bo resisted the urge to explain that Delilah Brasseur might be such an angel, and that Bo herself might be the agent divinely selected to carry the child out of harm's way. "Grandiose," such delusions were called. And that sense of divine mission—the dead giveaway of mania.

"Brasseur was the Rowes' housekeeper for years," Tally explained. "The old family retainer."

"She said she knew about Weppo," Bo went on. "She said she called 'the daddy' and he came and took Weppo. She was scared, really scared. She said . . ." Bo paused to control her voice, "it was all up to me."

"But how does she know *you?*" Tally pressed.

"I don't know. I left my card with the maid at the Rowes' house, but that wasn't Delilah Brasseur. I remember voices. The maid was a much younger woman."

"But the maid may have known Brasseur. Must have. The maid gave Brasseur your card, and she called you."

"I guess," Bo conceded. Reality was dull, compared to the delusionally divine voice on the answering machine.

"There is nothing but reality!" a familiar German accent warned inside her head.

"Okay, okay," Bo answered.

"Okay what?"

"Okay, so Brasseur called me," Bo hedged, "but we still don't know anything."

"She said it would be over by Tuesday. Tuesday's the election. The attacks on your Wilhelm back there have something to do with the election. Tia Rowe and the election. But what?"

Bo glanced at the car's padded ceiling. "You're asking me? Probably the only truly ripe candidate for four-point restraints for four hundred miles in any direction? All I know is, I had to save Weppo. I want him to learn ASL and go to Gallaudet and become the first deaf President of the United States."

"You're crazy," Tally nodded, "but you've got guts. I'm going to park you and the boy with your Indians, assuming we find them, and then get back to that pay phone. If we can get this story together we may just stop Tia Rowe."

Tally's headlights sliced the gloom of a silent main street and came to rest on a shabby, two-story hotel. Bo could see the place in its heyday, horses tethered in front, sun-hardened prospectors with gold nuggets in pouches tied secretly about their necks. Were there gold mines up here? She thought so. Lone Pine had the look of a mining town, its halcyon past obscured by layers of dust and faded paint.

"The hotel will have a night clerk," Tally noted sensibly. "He'll know where Garcia's street is."

Leaving the car running, she sprinted into the darkened building.

Bo tipped the mirror toward herself and pulled a brush through her hair. She didn't look that bad, she decided. Exhausted, but not wild-eyed wacko. Not yet. In shadows at the periphery of the mirror's reflection, something moved. Bo spun around in time to see the rear wheels of a car vanish around a corner. No taillights. The car's lights weren't on. Why would somebody be driving around musty little Lone Pine, California, in the middle of the night with no lights on? Terror slammed through Bo like an iceberg surfacing from freezing, watery depths. It was them! It had to be.

Sliding into the driver's seat, Bo put the car in gear and honked. Behind a dust-filmed second-story window a light flickered on, and then off again.

"Get in!" Bo yelled as Gretchen Tally emerged from the hotel's lobby, puzzled. "They're here!"

"Who's here?" Tally questioned, diving into the moving car.

"The killers. It's them. I saw a car back there behind us, in the mirror. With no lights on. They're here!"

Tally's look was wary, sympathetic.

"I don't see any car. I think you're imagining it. Try to calm down. I've got directions to this Charlie Garcia's house. And there is a pow-wow going on, so we may have the right place—"

"I'm not imagining it!" Bo insisted.

"Okay. Turn right at this corner and follow the road two miles up into the hills. Then there's a dirt road called Coyote Spur that goes off to the right."

Bo flipped off the lights and propelled the car up a long, open grade toward the hulking foothills beyond.

"Indians say that mountains walk at night," she mentioned. Ahead the purple-gray forms seemed to waken, shudder a little as if throwing off sleep. For one of them to have moved, hugely and slowly, off toward Death Valley to the east, or north toward Mono Lake with its jagged salt-crystal pillars jutting from murky water, would not have surprised Bo. Walking mountains might just be a part of nature. Killing children was not.

Tally jotted notes furiously in a tiny spiral notebook.

"So, you found a receipt from Jamail's on the ground near where the child was abandoned, right?"

"Yeah," Bo replied vaguely. The hills stretching west from Lone Pine were two hundred million years old, she remembered from a ranger's lecture during her last visit. The number was incomprehensible. Nothing could really matter, in comparison to such vast age.

"And after the attack on the boy in the hospital you flew to Houston where you were told by a clerk at Jamail's that the receipt bore an accounting code designating the Rowes.

Then you went to the Rowe mansion in River Oaks where you gave your card to a maid and left. Is that right?''

"Right," Bo answered flatly.

The reporter's words didn't really tell the story. The words seemed silly, pointless.

"I saw billboards for Tia Rowe," she tried to explain. "Her eyes... there's something wrong with her. She isn't... human."

"If you start telling me Tia Rowe's an alien from an old *Star Trek* segment or something, I'm going to have to assume you're not what we call a reliable informant." Tally grimaced. "I'm going to have to assume I'm out in the middle of God-knows-where with a seriously disturbed woman who has kidnapped a child. I am, in fact, an accessory to that kidnapping. You're not going to tell me Tia's an invader from the Crab Nebula, are you, Bo?''

"No," Bo answered. "Nothing like that."

People, she acknowledged for perhaps the millionth time in her life, brought a different measure to bear on things said by those with psychiatric histories. You had to be coldly precise, avoid colorful turns of phrase. Or else there would be the meaningful exchange of glances, after which you would be dismissed like a quaint but useless toy. And even the trustworthy Gretchen Tally was one of "them," the ones who held the reins of reality.

"I am convinced," Bo stated in the unpunctuated syntax of a computer-generated voice, "that Weppo was in that house until Delilah Brasseur discovered something that led her to believe he was in great danger. She called Weppo's father to come and rescue him. I think the father stole a car in Houston and then drove to San Diego and hid out for a few days with Weppo in a shack on the Barona Reservation. I think the father tied Weppo to a mattress there and then left, meaning to come back. But he never came back because he died from an overdose of some street drug.''

"You sound like a computer,'' Tally said, cringing. "It gives me the creeps. But I think you're right. I think Weppo's father was Kep Rowe. My editor's checking it out with the San Diego Police. Kep's been arrested in Houston, more than once, on drug charges. The prints are being faxed to San Diego right now. If it's Kep, we have a story.''

"Why would somebody want to kill Tia Rowe's grandson?'' Bo asked, shaving a right turn onto a dirt road identified as Coyote Spur only by a whitewash sign painted on a boulder.

"The question is,'' Tally pondered, "why didn't anybody know there was a Rowe grandchild?''

"Wild oats,'' Bo guessed. "An illegitimate child. Isn't that the sort of thing they still cover up in the South?''

"Maybe,'' the reporter conceded. "But Delilah Brasseur called Kep to get the child away from danger in Houston. That means the child was in Houston to begin with. Hidden in Houston. But from what? What for? And where's the mother?''

Amid a roughly circular jumble of granite outcroppings Bo discerned a cinder-block house surrounded by cars and pickup trucks. Some of the trucks had camper shells. Others were parked to shelter tents from the wind. The pow-wow.

"I don't know anything more than I've told you,'' Bo droned.

The landscape might have been the moon.

"I hope this is the right place,'' Tally said. "Are you sure these Indians will let you and Weppo stay? Will you be safe?''

"We aren't safe anyplace,'' Bo replied. "But Annie will help. I know she will.''

As Bo eased the car quietly among the parked vehicles, a

shape moved near the back of the house. An ancient woman in long skirts and a man's overcoat. She moved slowly out of the shadows and then merely stood in the moonlit circle of rocks.

Bo was suddenly aware that the dreamlike enclosure contained not one, but fifty pairs of eyes, alert and watchful. The somnambulant scene masked a deep interest, and a sympathy palpable in the air. They'd been waiting. Annie Garcia and her people had known they were coming, and waited in silence.

In a trance Bo gathered the sleeping child from Tally's car, and approached the old woman.

"Good luck," the reporter whispered.

Bo nodded, as Gretchen Tally slid into the driver's seat and turned to leave.

"Welcome," Annie Garcia pronounced softly. "I knew you would come. There is still much danger, or you wouldn't have driven here. My grandson Charlie, he knows a place to hide."

Bo watched as a sleeping truck stirred and moved toward her. Behind its wheel was a man with Annie's cheekbones and wide skull, but much younger.

"There are coats, blankets, food ready for you," he said. "Get in. We will hide you."

Bo held Weppo warmly against her body as Annie Garcia's grandson edged the truck out a dirt trail toward the hills to the north. In the alkaline, moon-washed landscape Bo searched for Lois Bittner's reality and did not find it.

What she found was planetary rubble. A forsaken wasteland where things infinitely older than the boned jellyfish named "human" breathed and had life. What could this be, if not a pattern in which she was merely a function? Bo felt herself rocking slightly. The comforting, primitive motion of the very young, the very old, and the very disturbed.

"We'll be there in about half an hour," the man said. "Mine shafts, up in these hills, you could hide in them forever."

The word echoed like light on the senseless jumble of rocks outside. "Forever, forever." It would be all right, to live among the moon-torn rocks. To become something else, go back to a crystalline self deep inside, be a stone.

Weppo stirred against her, his warm head pushing at her chest.

But not him. He has to have a life. You've got to hang on, for him.

After a while the truck ground to a halt on a hill amid other, identical hills, shining and lost.

"Up there." The man pointed to a small hole in a landslide of rocky debris. "You can hide. No one will find you. When it is safe, we will come for you."

Bo struggled into a leather jacket and shouldered the backpack Charlie Garcia handed her. Weppo whined groggily as she stuffed him into another jacket and slung him over her shoulder. He clung to her like a peevish monkey.

As the truck pulled away she wondered what Lois Bittner would say about all this, and laughed. On a rock near the opening of the mine tunnel scuttled a figure she would have sworn was her dead sister, Laurie.

33

Desert Shadows

Andrew LaMarche sucked air through his teeth and watched the road below. A few cars, pickups, an occasional eighteen-wheeler hauling produce the hard, mountainous way to Nevada. So far no faded blue BMW propelled by a wild Irishwoman with a deaf child.

At intervals the helicopter's pilot zagged off into the desert and swept searchlights over the monotonous desolation, as if actually looking for something amid the chollas and broken granite. It was a ruse suggested by Rudy Palachek, to explain the presence of a USMC helicopter trailing a public road in the middle of the night. Any observer, even an official one like the California Highway Patrol, would assume they were a search patrol on federal orders, probably tracking a drug run out of Mexico. Swooping searchlights and the slicing churn of helicopter rotors were common nocturnal events in Southern California. No one, except those for whom the lights searched, took much notice.

LaMarche surveyed the desert landscape somberly. A

bizarre terrain of mineral rubbish and resinous, spiky plants. Sharp shadows laid by the full moon made a black-silver crazy quilt of the ground below. How would this look to Bo? To a woman grappling with an octopuslike mania whose embrace would only exaggerate the desert's eeriness? And those hideous Joshua trees. They looked, he remembered from a microbiology lab, like the tentacled freshwater organisms called hydras. Sea serpents named in Greek mythology. When Hercules hacked off one of their nine heads, two replaced it. A dry sea, peopled by monsters. Is that how Bo would see this? Was she terrified, alone with the boy out here? Unaccustomed to imaginative thought, he found it rather enjoyable. But Bo wouldn't. Not now.

"Wait a minute," Rudy Palachek yelled above the rotors. "I think we've got something."

LaMarche noted Palachek's broad hand drop to clasp the butt of an M-14 rifle on the floor. A Leupold Vari-X III sniper scope mounted on the barrel would give Rudy a distinct advantage over men armed with handguns. And in the cool, moonlit desert there would be no distortion from heat mirages. Rudy Palachek could pick off a cowboy killer from a long, long way. And given the chance, he would.

But the car below them was deserted. Abandoned at the edge of the road. The helicopter leaned into a circle and landed on packed sand thirty feet away.

LaMarche scuttled under the whipping blades and approached the silent car, Rudy following. Beneath his right hand the hood was cool.

"They've been gone for at least an hour, probably more," he yelled.

Rudy tried a door, then stood back and blew out a rear window with the M-14.

In the glass-littered interior LaMarche found crayons, coloring books, and a drawing of a taco, done in blue.

Napkins from a Mexican restaurant in San Diego. A dozen or so cassette tapes, most of them Bach. The odor of French cigarettes and shampoo. He felt like a sneak thief, some scurrilous invader in a private space that belonged to a woman who was a stranger. A woman who loved Bach and would risk her life to protect a nameless child. He would like, he realized, to be invited into the life of such a woman. More than that, he would be honored. But first he had to find her. If she were still alive.

"Looks like somebody else's been here," Rudy Palachek shouted, pointing to tracks in the sandy shoulder behind Bo's car. The clear outline of tire treads. Bare patches in gravelly debris indicating foot traffic. But no blood. No cratered holes where bullets exploded. And no tracks leading into the desert.

"Somebody caught up with her here, but didn't kill her," LaMarche theorized. "But who? Why? Why would she leave her car and go with somebody? The killers would've shot them both right here. It was somebody else."

"Tank's empty," Rudy noted after checking with a creosote bush branch. "She ran out of gas. Maybe somebody just picked them up. Who wouldn't? A woman and a kid out here? Anybody'd stop, give them a ride."

Bo had let her car run out of gas. Why? LaMarche couldn't make sense of it. She'd had the presence of mind to feed the child, even provide toys for him. How could she forget to fuel a car that was their only means of escape?

"She'll get to Lone Pine, to that Indian woman," he decided aloud. "If she's hitchhiking now with the boy, that's still where she'll go."

"We'll be there in twenty minutes," Palachek predicted, tight-lipped. "But the bullet-boys are ahead of us. Let's go!"

As the helicopter climbed noisily out of rock-strewn nothingness LaMarche experienced an awareness that his entire life since Sylvie's death might be compared to this desert. But no longer.

34

Dead End

The shape that might have been Laurie, or might have been a trick of moonshine and breathless shadow, vanished between the time Bo looked down to assure her footing on the pebbly ground and then looked up again. Her heartbeat was rapid; she felt a little dizzy from the climb toward the small dark niche in the hillside above. But that was okay. Always okay to walk, climb, move. Necessary, even.

Behind the hill the moon had passed its zenith and begun its slide down the back of the sky. A warning. The approach of the nightly down time, a dead zone hidden like an egg inside every cycle of darkness. A time when even things of the night cease their howling, their swift, padded movement across a million paths lacing the desert. The hours of terror in which nothing moves.

Except in certain little-known places, Bo thought. Well-lit nurses' stations like beacons in silent psychiatric corridors. Oases of light where one disheveled sufferer in pajamas after another will congregate briefly, chat about last night's movie or tomorrow's breakfast menu as if it were perfectly ordinary to exchange pleasantries at 3:00 A.M. The hunger for the sound of a human voice. A need for reassurance. Never so great as in those who cannot sleep through those hollow hours.

But there would be no friendly psychiatric aide here. No night nurse willing to put aside the charts and prattle about an article in *Time* or where to get the best deal on radial tires. Here there were only boulders, rocks, stones of every imaginable composition—an exhalation of matter older than breath itself. And the dead weight of a sleeping child.

You will do precisely what the Indian said, Bradley. You will hide.

The climb up the spill of rubble to the mine tunnel was treacherous. Every foothold created a dusty avalanche of rock that sounded like a shooting gallery in the desert silence. Bo wondered if it mattered. There could be no one else in this wasteland, surely. Even the killers could not come here. And yet there was a sense of something, some*one*, watching. A watcher in the dead hours? Impossible. But it was there. And no more inexplicable, Bo realized, than the fact that she was there. Some conscious thing, sharing this barren realm.

Bo controlled a whole-body tremor of fear. Held it tightly inside the muscles of her back, her stomach.

No panic. Absolutely none!

Hauling Weppo and the backpack over the rim of the tunnel, she collapsed inside. Silence. No dripping limestone cavern this, with milky stalactites hanging from its ceilings. Just a hollow tube snaked into the hill for access to its veins, its gold, iron, lead. Metallic veins, sluiced through depths of earth before pterodactyls swooped in steaming skies. Before the earth cooled and wrinkled, throwing up these mountains like creases in a blanket. Just a mining tunnel. Quiet and safe.

Bo took a measure of her surroundings. The tunnel was oval, with a flat floor. About six feet high. No supporting timbers. Rocks, some rounded and some jagged, protruded at every conceivable angle from the reamed interior of the hill. Most bore a yellowish cast, orangey brown striations. A scent of iron.

Unfastening the blanket tied beneath the pack, Bo lay it on the tunnel's floor and carefully placed Weppo on it. Wakened somewhat by the jerky climb, he regarded her blearily. Bo pointed to a mottled yellow-brown rock at his head.

"Rock," she signed with the right-fist-banging-back-of-left-fist gesture every child learned in the Scissors, Paper, Rock game. "We—are—in—a—rock—house."

Weppo nodded.

"Na-na," he crooned against the rough blanket. "Na-na."

In sleep he pronounced the traditional grandmotherly endearment comfortably. So he'd had a nana who'd taught him to call her that, to pronounce two inaudible syllables out loud. Probably so he could call to her. So she could hear him. But who?

If Gretchen Tally were right, Tia Rowe was Weppo's grandmother. Bo could not, even in manic reaches of imagination, picture the reptile-eyed senatorial candidate as a nana. Some things could not *be*, period. This was one of them.

Then like a remembered bar of a Bach concerto, a deep voice sang, ". . . I know about the baby, the little boy. . ." Delilah Brasseur! That voice was Nana's. Bo would have bet on it. The fondness there. The love.

Resting beside the sleeping child, her back against an outcropping of fool's gold, Bo made an effort to relax. Stretched. Shrugged the knotted muscles in her shoulders.

Scratched her head. It didn't work. Inactivity would produce its own entertainment. The manic brain detests boredom.

On the tunnel's bouldery walls Bo saw flickers. Dull, smudgy pinlights that vanished when she moved her head, only to reveal others. Mostly near the tunnel's opening, where the moon's light still drifted. Fool's gold again. Traces of iron pyrite feebly reflecting the light. The tunnel was actually fascinating.

With a cigarette lighter found in the leather jacket she created a bubble of gold haze that caught and shined on a million surfaces. Gritrock, porphyry, gneiss. Mentally she recited forgotten terms from a geology class. Was there pumice here? She could do her nails. And ironstone. There would be ironstone. The place smelled like a foundry. And the tiny yellow sparkles? Not pyrite but cairngorm. The yellow quartz of which her grandmother had a bracelet, each stone etched in a Celtic design. Each stone in the bracelet a story. Like a rosary.

In the undulating shadows beyond the bubble of light Bo thought she saw a photograph, embedded somehow in granite. A photograph of Laurie before she died. Laurie signing something, trying to tell her something. Laurie before the gray dress and the lace collar, so still. Laurie in herringbone corduroys and a baggy Irish sweater, signing. But wait. Those were her clothes, the ones she'd worn when it all started. When she saw Weppo and knew he was deaf.

Her thumb jerked away from the overheated lighter, and darkness swallowed the apparition. Sucking the burn, she tried to read the signs in her mind. But they made no sense. Was it Laurie's spirit? How would Laurie's spirit find her here? Weppo shifted his weight on the rocky floor, stretching the Indian blanket like a moth in a cocoon. Of course! Laurie could find her through Weppo. Two deaf children, connected in silence. Except that one of them wasn't a child, wasn't even alive. But would that matter? Laurie had been a child when Bo left for college, and never went back. Only ten. Laurie's spirit had come to tell Bo it was okay. Okay to have walked away in shame from a little sister your friends called "retard." Okay to have forgotten birthdays. Okay even not to ask a shy, awkward fifteen-year-old to be in your wedding.

Bo flipped the lighter on again and saw only rocks where Laurie had been. No moving photograph. Just the sameness of rocks, any hundred of which might replace another hundred, and change nothing.

"There is nothing but reality," Lois Bittner pronounced as clearly as if she'd been sitting there.

So this was reality. Rocks.

You're sitting in a tunnel near Lone Pine. You're hiding here with Weppo until it's safe, and Annie's grandson comes. Laurie is dead. Weppo isn't. Move around. Keep your grip.

Bo stood and walked carefully into the tunnel's depth, turning to check on the sleeping child at every other step. A fresh breeze alerted her to the presence of another corridor a hundred and fifty yards inside the hill, even before she came to it. A shorter, rougher cloister than the one in which Weppo slept soundly, it angled down through the hill's north face and afforded a view of the dirt road on which, Bo assumed, they'd come here. Through the noose of light at the shorter tunnel's end Bo saw something odd on the road. Something darker than rock, with unrocklike angles. A car.

Hurrying soundlessly to the opening, Bo lay flat and peered out. It was a car, just sitting there. No one in it. No one around.

Then she saw, emerging from within another tunnel in the hill across the road, the bright yellow-blue glare of a butane lantern. It signaled to someone nearby. Someone on the hillside beneath her. Someone in a Stetson hat, searching her hill for openings.

Bo's heart shrank to a whine in her chest.

Don't scream. Whatever you do, don't scream. And don't light the lighter. Don't make any noise. Get Weppo and run into the hill. It's honeycombed with tunnels. They won't find you. They can't!

Panicked, Bo stumbled over a rock and fell hard on both hands. A searing pain shot through her right wrist. Her hand grew wet. Blood. But her fingers still moved. She'd torn her hand open, but the wrist wasn't broken.

Great! Now you'll bleed to death. Tie it up with something but keep moving. This is it. The last chance.

Bo tugged violently at her sweatshirt and found that it wouldn't rip. The leather jacket then. Its lining tore out easily, and she knotted it about her hand while running. But the nylon did little to stop the dripping blood.

You might as well leave a trail of breadcrumbs. They'll see the damn blood.

Weppo, wakened roughly by the scoop of Bo's arms, kicked and thrashed.

"Shhh," she whispered against the wiry head.

Pointless. He couldn't hear. And he began to scream. A croaking scream, ululant and loonlike. Bo had heard it all her life.

There was nothing to do but run. Run in the darkness through ragged stone that clutched and tore. Holding the writhing child with her left arm, she felt the tunnel wall with her right. A huge, directionless Braille that gave no instructions. Her hand was still bleeding. Behind her she heard a male voice—"In here!" And something else.

Footsteps behind, closer than the voice. That sense of another presence. Laurie. It had to be Laurie, tagging after her as usual. The croaking shriek.

The tunnel angled uphill, grew smaller. Bo hunched to avoid granite shrapnel lurking above her head, invisible in the dark. The footsteps, Laurie's footsteps, followed.

"Go away!" Bo yelled as she'd done a thousand times. "You're a pest. Leave me alone!"

Her right hand, she realized with a curl of pain, was signing the words as she said them.

A dim light ahead signaled another tunnel, running down to the right, to the hill's south face. Partially collapsed, it allowed no way out. Above four feet of rubble in its center Bo could see a claw of sky, and hear a sound like a giant, slow-moving jackhammer. The sound seemed to be coming down from the sky. Were they drilling into the hill? Planting dynamite? Were they going to blow up the hill, blast all the tunnels shut, leave them inside to die? What else could they be doing with a jackhammer? The sound died as she listened.

Then the male voice, closer.

"She's goin' this way. Piece of cake!"

Scrabbling up the narrowing main passageway, now a stifling trough, Bo realized her mistake. The tunnel was ending! She should have tried to get over the pile of slag in the collapsed tunnel. At least stuffed Weppo over it, given him one last chance for life.

Edging the final inches to the tunnel's jagged end, Bo crammed Weppo behind her and blocked him with her body. Then, kicking and clawing at the walls, she tried to bring the little chamber down on them. Bury them in granite rubbish that might deflect the poison bullets, buy enough time for Charlie Garcia to come. For someone to come. But the hill, undisturbed beyond this point, held firm, packed by aeons of pressure. A few rocks broke loose and fell, but too few to bury them.

Scraping the debris before her into a pile, she heard

Weppo's scream, felt the presence of the other. Of Laurie, who wouldn't go away. Who was going to have to die twice.

This isn't what was supposed to happen. Not this.

Cowering behind the little rock pile, Weppo screaming, hysterical at her back, Bo saw yellow-blue light fill the space she had traversed in darkness. A man behind the light. Skinny. Short. Bent in the narrow space. In his right hand a gun with a black cylinder at the end. Grinning.

"Up here!" he yelled over his shoulder. "Ya can hear the dummy!"

With her bloody hand Bo found a jagged stone and wrapped her fingers around it. He hadn't seen her yet. She still had one nearly hopeless chance. Moving from behind the pile of rubble to give her arm enough room to throw, she placed herself squarely in his view.

But Laurie thought of it first.

Leaping from the bend of the south-facing tunnel, the ghost of her sister threw an arc of grit and pebbles into the man's face. Then a blast rang out in circles, shaking dirt, dust, rock from the walls.

Bo saw the crumpled figure on the tunnel floor. Familiar. Wearing a skirt she might have worn in junior high. But it wasn't Laurie. The hair was white and wild. The skull wide. The skin darker than any Irish girl's, and weathered like old wood. In the chest was a gaping crater from which Annie Garcia's life drained in silent streams.

"*Nooooo!*" a scream ripped from Bo's throat as she threw the rock in her hand. It hit the man in the neck. He snarled, lifted the gun, and then fell as half his head flew in shreds to splatter the primordial walls. Something, a sound, reverberated like a whirlwind through the space, pulling dirt and rock loose in showers. It had been another shot. More massive than the last. Deadly to the man with the gun.

Bo could not close her eyes, could not stop a palsy that

turned her legs to sand. Shaking, she leaned against Weppo and merely breathed as Rudy Palachek stumbled through the murky, dust-filled tunnel, a rifle in his hand.

"Ms. Bradley?" he said with irrational courtesy, "It's okay. We got the other one, right back there." He gestured with the rifle. "With a knife. Cut him up a little, while Andy broke his wrist to get the gun. But he'll live to talk. Don't worry. You can come out now. Bring the boy on out. It's okay. Charlie Garcia brought us here in time."

Bo tried to move and could not. Every muscle was locked. Her whole body a soundless scream that could not move. Behind her Weppo's shrieks faded hoarsely.

"I scream because I am a bird." The Paiute chant filled her ears as she stared at the old woman on the stony floor.

"The boy will rise up."

As tears blurred her vision, Bo began to rock. Just slightly, but enough to break the paralysis. Weppo crept under her arm and then clung to her, rocking softly at her side.

"Uhhhh," Bo tried to speak, but the sound emerged in a croak.

From behind Rudy, Andrew LaMarche emerged, breathless in a rattle of pebbles.

"Oh, God," he whispered. "Bo. It's all right. You saved him. Look. He's right there next to you. He's alive. And so are you."

Bo felt the warm, small body beside her, felt it rise and run to Rudy Palachek, who grabbed the boy in huge arms and hugged him. In the boy's face she saw Laurie smile briefly, and then vanish.

Andrew LaMarche was holding her, pulling her gently from the jagged crevice she'd thought would be her grave. And Weppo's.

"Come on," he urged quietly. "Let's get you outside. It will be better outside."

On her feet now, Bo stopped to touch Annie Garcia's face. Even in death the old eyes showed no fear, only that mysterious ferocity, now visibly waning, which was in Bo's experience the signature of those who live fully. Closing the bronze eyelids with her own pale, freckled hand, Bo thought she felt the spirit of the Indian envelop her one last time before the eclipse of death. In the tunnel's chill air Bo sensed a retreating notion her people called Cally Berry— Caillech Bera, the irrefutable truth of death. Somberly Bo stood and allowed herself to be led out the long tunnel. From inside the ancient walls she thought she heard the voice of a little girl who had never talked saying, "Bye, Bo. It's okay now. I know you loved me. Bye."

35

Holy Innocents

Tia Rowe woke somewhat earlier than her usual 6:00 A.M. and rose to open embroidered drapes, refreshed by a sound, untroubled sleep. The girl she hired after Deely left had vanished as well, but no matter. Skiltia Marievski knew how to make her own coffee. And her own future.

Striding to the kitchen in an ecru silk dressing gown that deepened the butterscotch color of her eyes, she glanced at her answering machine. The retarded child had inherited her eyes, the Marievski eyes she remembered flashing from her aging father's face when he told her what he'd done.

"You hated us from the day you were born," he raged. "You broke your mother's heart with your hate. I pity you because you can feel no love, but I will not place the fruit of my life's work in your hands. You will inherit nothing from me! The paintings, my entire estate will be held in trust for my grandchildren, Kep and Julie, and for their children. Nothing for you, Skiltia, because you have given us nothing!"

The old man died three weeks later.

What a fool, to think she wouldn't get what she wanted in the end.

But the answering machine wasn't blinking. No one had called during the night. They should have called, left the coded message that would tell her it was over. Tell her the monstrous child, the mistake standing between her and twenty-six million dollars, was dead.

Well, they'd call eventually. No point in wasting time worrying about it. Tia Rowe warmed a croissant in the toaster oven and assessed the best possible use of the morning.

Sunday. Hard to accomplish much on a Sunday. People were at church . . . church! Perfect.

Tia drank her coffee and set the Quimper cup back in its saucer briskly. An early mass. The widow alone, seeking solace and strength in prayer. She'd wear black, of course, but not the Givenchy. That would be for the funeral home this afternoon. Something tailored, then? No. Something blousy, feminine. Something to suggest a heart broken with grief.

Finding a Roman Catholic church in the Yellow Pages, Tia left messages for two photographers designating the time and place, and then hurriedly found the gray silk blouse with poufs of white lace at the collar and cuffs. Under the black cape it would be fine.

Twenty minutes later she saw one of the photographers lounging in a car parked across the street from the rectory of Holy Innocents Church. He ambled from the car as she parked her Mercedes near a cluster of young Georgia pines bounding the church property. A handful of people, well dressed and quiet, chatted briefly on the little church's flagstone steps before entering. Tia covered her head with the cape's hood and ignored the photographer as she walked demurely toward the open doors.

"Mrs. Rowe?" he called as she expected. The surprise photo, caught by a vigilant journalist at an unusual moment.

Tia looked somberly from beneath her cape at the young man beside the steps.

"Yes?"

"You're under arrest," came a voice from behind her as two of the well-dressed men lingering on the church steps pulled her arms back and snapped handcuffs over poufs of white lace.

The photographer caught the picture, framed by church doors.

"There's been some mistake," Tia Rowe pronounced urgently. "You can't do this!"

"No mistake, ma'am," came the calm reply. "If you'll just come with us now..."

It couldn't be happening! The plan had been foolproof. Nothing to it. Just get rid of that wretched child, inherit the money, and win the election. Anything, Tia had known, could be bought. Money was all that mattered. Money, and power! She'd almost had both.

"Your hired boys got caught," the HPD officer mentioned while handing Tia carefully into a waiting squad car, "up in some California hill country. One of them's dead. The other one talked. And the boy... well he's just fine."

The boy. Tia's mind wrenched, turned on itself in a paroxysm of hate. An idiot she should have suffocated at birth! Because of that thing she'd kept in her attic, it was over. Senseless, that her plans would be wasted because of a brain-damaged, subhuman monster whose life could accomplish nothing.

"I demand to speak with my attorney immediately," she told the squad car's uniformed driver.

"At the station, ma'am," he answered.

Behind them the heavy oak doors of Holy Innocents Church swung shut.

36

Weppo

Bo woke slowly with a headache she recognized immediately as a sedative hangover. In a bed. Clean sheets. Ugly orange-flowered bedspread, but not of the serviceable twill universally selected by psychiatric hospitals. Maybe she wasn't in a hospital. Then why were there flowers everywhere?

Through narrowed eyes she found the window. Ugly orange curtains to match the bedspread. But no bars.

Okay, it's not a hospital, but what is it? Where are you? And where's Weppo?

With an effort that sent dull spikes of pain through her bandaged hand she pulled herself up on an elbow and was stunned to see Estrella Benedict in a chair beside the bed, grinning.

"Es? What are you doing here? Where am I? Where's Weppo?"

Estrella appeared to be caught somewhere between tears and laughter. "Dr. LaMarche called early this morning. Henry and I drove up right away. You've been asleep all day. We're in Bishop, forty miles north of Lone Pine. It was the only place LaMarche could find a decent motel.''

So it was a motel. Of course. Where else would you find plastic ''Mediterranean'' furniture with reproduction prints of Death Valley under snow? Bo felt tears spilling from her eyes.

''I thought . . .'' she began.

''No, no,'' her office mate crooned, hugging her. ''You're not in a hospital. LaMarche sedated you himself. Everything's all right. You just need to rest for a few weeks, take your lithium. It's all under control. And wait until you hear what that reporter—''

''Weppo.'' Bo remembered. ''Where's Weppo?''

Estrella smoothed Bo's unruly hair. ''Haven't you heard of creme rinse?'' She laughed. ''Weppo's fine. Off somewhere with Rudy, seeing the sights. I think they're playing miniature golf at the moment. Don't worry. It's over.''

Bo thought of the mining tunnel, Annie Garcia on its floor with a hole in her chest.

''Annie's dead,'' she pronounced. ''I thought she was Laurie, but . . .''

''Try not to go over and over what happened,'' Estrella warned. ''Orders from LaMarche's sister in Louisiana. A shrink or something. He's been on the phone with her for hours, trying to figure out what to do with you . . .''

''*Do* with me!'' Bo fumed. ''Why in hell does he need to *do* with me?''

She was on her feet in spite of the headache.

''Because he wants to.'' Estrella grinned. ''I think he likes you, Bo.''

''How flattering,'' Bo sniped.

Es merely grinned lasciviously. ''About time, Bo.''

In a small refrigerator under the luggage shelf Bo found

fruit juice, chocolate eclairs, and Cokes. Estrella handed her a bottle of aspirin.

"Who did all this?" Bo asked, including the flowers with a sweep of her bandaged hand.

"LaMarche. Annie's grandson. That reporter, Gretchen Tally. Everybody. You're a hero. Everybody wants to do things for you."

"What about Madge?" Bo remembered reality with a lurch. "I suppose I'm out of a job."

"Nope. Thanks to your reporter from Houston. God, she's good! Threatened Madge with nationwide coverage— 'San Diego Department of Social Services Fires Top Investigator Who Saved Deaf Boy from Hired Gunmen! Film at Eleven!' Madge went belly-up when she realized sacking you would hurt the department's image. She even decided you have a work-related injury justifying three weeks' paid sick leave. LaMarche thought of that. *Muy astuto*, huh?"

"*Muy*," Bo agreed. It was overwhelming.

"And that woman who called you from Houston?" Estrella went on with enthusiasm. "Delilah Brasseur?"

Bo remembered. "Does she know Weppo's okay? Has anybody told her?" The nana would be frantic.

"Tally's paper got a message to her through the preacher at her church. She was hiding out someplace, from that *woman . . .*"

"Tia Rowe," Bo pronounced. The unanswered question.

"Those flowers are from Brasseur," Estrella pointed to a bouquet of pink carnations and baby's breath on the night-stand. Bo opened the card.

"Bless you," it said simply, "from Deely Brasseur."

Bo sank back onto the bed. The aspirins were helping the headache, but also reminding her that she hadn't eaten anything but seven-grain bread in twenty-four hours. She hoped never to see another slice of seven-grain bread in her life.

A commotion in the hall alerted Estrella, who rose to answer the door.

"That'll be the crew." She smiled. "I'm glad you're okay, Bo. That office would've been a frigging pit without you."

A small boy in a large red-and-gold sweatshirt with "USMC" embossed across the chest bounded across the room and into Bo's arms.

"I love you!" she signed, and hugged him hard, unable to let go.

He squirmed in her arms and then looked questioning.

"Food?" he signed, grinning.

A bright little boy. Happy. Hungry.

Reality. Lois Bittner was right. There could be nothing better. How could anyone have wanted to snuff this young life, obliterate it, kill it?

Rudy Palachek, LaMarche, Henry Benedict, and Gretchen Tally poured in the door amid congratulations.

"You're one in a million!" Tally enthused. "I just came by to say goodbye. Got to get back to Houston, plan the coverage for Bea Yannick's win by default on Tuesday. People are going to say she didn't really win. She'll need our support."

Bo's confusion was evident. "I've been asleep all day," she said. "What's happened?"

"Tia's in the toilet!" the young reporter crowed. "Thanks to you, and Deely Brasseur, and your Paiute, Annie Garcia. The doctor'll fill in the details. I've got a commuter flight to San Francisco, leaves in twenty minutes. The connection'll have me back in Houston before midnight. And Bo," the young woman's look was sincere, "there will be nothing in the coverage of this story about your manic-depression, nothing that can hurt you.''

"I knew that," Bo offered in acknowledgment. "I knew you could be trusted, although I wish all this secrecy wasn't necessary. Nobody has to lie about having diabetes or glaucoma or even leprosy." Bo knew she was lecturing, and didn't care.

"I know, you're right," Tally interjected, leaving. "Someday people will let go of the idea that brain disorders are the work of the devil. What's important is that we stopped the *real* devil before she got away with it. See ya!"

"Tia Rowe is something out of Poe," Andrew LaMarche commented, closing the door. "According to my sister, she's what used to be called a sociopath—a person devoid of the ability for human closeness, loyalty, love. Incapable of anything but self-interest. Manipulative. Treacherous."

"I knew that when I saw her pictures on the billboards," Bo sighed. "But so what? Nobody locks them up."

"And nobody's going to lock you up," LaMarche stated with more emotion than he had intended. "Charlie Garcia insists that you and the boy attend some sort of memorial ceremony for Annie tonight. I don't think it's a good idea, but—"

"We'll be there," Bo answered. It felt right, the idea of joining in a ritual for the wise old woman whose life had touched hers and the child's so deeply. The wise old woman who had, literally, traded her life for theirs. "And then I need to go home, be left alone for a while until the lithium builds up to blood level, whatever that means," she went on. "I really want to avoid the hospital this time."

Andrew LaMarche looked so earnest he could have sold Bibles to penguins. Bo had to laugh.

"You don't understand," she said with a grin. "Mania is disturbing, embarrassing for everybody around, but it's not dangerous, at least not at first. You just can't sleep, you talk all the time, laugh and cry. Your thoughts fly out like wild birds from a cage. It's impossible to concentrate. You want to move around all the time. If it's let go, it gets scary. Psychotic. But I'm on the damn pills already. I'll be okay. It's the depression that's dangerous. People kill themselves rather than go through it one more time. A pain you can't imagine. That's when you need a hospital. Do you see?''

"Not really," LaMarche admitted. "But you know what you're talking about. I just want you to be all right."

The handsome, graying international authority on child abuse looked about as self-assured as a lost sheep. That look of confused concern found on faces that would *not* run in terror and revulsion from a schizophrenic daughter, a suicidally depressed husband. Bo had seen it before, but never for her. Never. Andrew LaMarche's look touched her so deeply she was afraid to cry, for fear she'd never stop.

"I'll be all right when I get something to eat besides bread," she joked, stifling the feeling.

Rudy Palachek extended a bearlike hand.

"Henry and I will go on back to San Diego now, in his car," he explained. "We'll stop at China Lake for your car and I'll drive it back to San Diego. The rest of you'll fly back on a charter tonight after the ceremony for Annie. I hope to see you again, Bo Bradley. I'm proud to know you."

Bo accepted the compliment with a nod of her head, and then flung her arms around the ruddy marine.

"You too, Henry." She hugged Estrella's husband through tears. "Thanks for bringing Es up to stay with me."

The emotional drain was too much. She had to lighten up or else lose it completely.

As the two men left, a phone on the desk began to ring. *What next?*

"Convent of the Perpetual Parakeet," Bo clowned to relieve the tension.

"Bo? This has to be you!"

Madge Aldenhoven's voice, chipper as a flea.

"It probably is, then," Bo replied. "Madge. I thought you'd never call."

"Dr. LaMarche said you'd wake up around six," the supervisor explained as if she'd never planned to relegate Bo to waiting in bread lines. "I'm glad we found a way around regulations. I'm glad you'll be coming back. We need you."

Manic or not, Bo was at a loss for words. Almost.

"What have you done with the *real* Madge Aldenhoven?" She laughed. "The shining light of bureaucracies everywhere?"

"Still here." Aldenhoven actually laughed in return. "And by the way, I thought you'd like to know—Angela Reavey's going to be okay. See you in three weeks!"

"The world is strange," Bo said, and then signed for Weppo, "Let's go eat."

Over dinner LaMarche explained the Marievski inheritance that Tia Rowe's father had earmarked for his grand children.

"The amount has quadrupled since the artist's death," LaMarche noted. "There's been a resurgence of interest in his work. Originals are going at auction now for seven figures. And Weppo now owns *hundreds* of originals."

The artist great-grandfather, from whom the child had inherited talent as well as those caramel-colored eyes.

"And was Kep Rowe the father? Was he the dead addict in the stolen car like Gretchen Tally thought?"

"Yes on both counts," LaMarche replied and then looked down, anticipating Bo's next question.

"And the mother...?" she asked.

"Weppo's mother is dead," he answered softly. "She

was Julie Rowe, Kep's sister. She died giving birth to him at home, in an attic where Tia had hidden her so no one would know of the pregnancy. Tia wasn't about to let this new obstacle to the Marievski fortune be known. But Deely Brasseur was there. She told all this to Gretchen Tally on the phone this afternoon, while you were asleep.''

LaMarche took a deep breath and went on.

"Tia Rowe never knew Kep was Weppo's father. Julie lied about it, made up a name. Only Deely knew the truth. That's why she called Kep when she overheard Tia telling a creditor she'd be coming into a fortune in the near future. Deely saw bags of quicklime stacked in the garage. She'd suspected all along that Tia might kill the child once her husband, Mac, was out of the way. When Tia fired her, Deely knew exactly what Tia planned to do.''

Bo began to shake, and hugged herself to stop it.

"Quicklime?"

"Don't think about it," Estrella urged. "Just *don't!* Look. He's right here and he's okay.''

Weppo, wolfing down a burger and fries, signed good enthusiastically, over and over.

Bo remembered the incongruous aluminum vent in the eaves of the Rowe mansion. More had gone on in that attic than could be measured.

"That inhuman mother, an alcoholic father," Estrella pondered, "the two teenagers just turned to each other for love when there was none anywhere else, and the result is Weppo.''

"Yes," Bo said, smiling across the Formica table at the pale child. "But his real name is Wilhelm. From now on, let's call him Willy.''

"Willy it is," LaMarche boomed happily. "And by the way, Bo, I've contacted my attorney in San Diego. I've applied for guardianship for Wep—for Willy. The paperwork will be filed in court first thing tomorrow morning. Aldenhoven didn't seem to think there'd be any problem with DSS. Rudy and his wife, Mary, will care for our boy until we can find good foster parents . . ."

"*Deaf* foster parents," Bo insisted. "A home where everybody signs, and we can visit him."

"I'll leave that up to you." LaMarche grinned.

She could do it, network with every deaf association in California, find a young couple who'd love and share their lives with the little boy. There was an excellent ASL school near San Francisco . . . and then Gallaudet!

"He probably *won't* be the first deaf president," she mused aloud. "He's an artist. But he'll be in the *best* galleries."

LaMarche and Estrella laughed.

It was going to be all right!

37

The Cry-Dance

From the turnoff onto Coyote Spur leading to Charlie
Garcia's house, Bo could see the flames. Vapor trails of
leaping orange that turned to smoke and climbed skyward.
As LaMarche eased the rental car to a halt near the collection of parked vehicles, shapes of dancers were visible. A
circle of people, bundled against the cold, shuffling in a
circle counterclockwise around the fire. An old man's voice,
chanting in a language Bo had never heard. Hypnotic, the
voice tones rising at the end of each phrase and then
beginning again. Over and over. A sad, peaceful sound.

As Estrella carried the curious child from the car's backseat
and Bo pulled on the leather jacket she'd worn in the tunnel,
a figure broke from the circle of dancers and approached.

Charlie Garcia in a plaid wool jacket and feather-banded
hat.

"It is an honor that you have come," he addressed Bo
formally. "This is my grandmother's cry-dance, the Paiute
way of releasing the spirit of one who has gone. My
grandmother hid on the truck, to stay with you and the boy,

to defend you. She knew she would die; she had known for a long time. This was the task of her spirit, and she performed it well. Her story, your story, will be told by our children to their children. Because of this, you and the boy are invited to dance with us.''

Bo felt a surge of warmth, of light within her that drew her toward the fire.

''Thank you,'' she said simply, and took the child now called Willy from Estrella's arms and set him on the ground beside her.

''Dance,'' she signed for him, circling two fingers downward over her open left palm. ''We—dance.''

Charlie escorted them toward the fire-lit circle where one somber face after another nodded acknowledgment. The dancers, every other one a man, a woman, a boy, a girl, made room in the circle for Bo and the child. He caught on to the shuffling step easily, and watched the fire as he danced. Bo felt self-conscious at first, but relaxed when she realized no one was watching anymore. They were all lost in the dance, the sonorous, repetitive chant.

From time to time, someone would cry, or make a yipping sound that rose with the smoke into moonlit skies. Across the circle Bo saw Maria and Joe Bigger Fox who would have driven to Lone Pine that morning after hearing of Annie's death. Like many of the dancers, they held in their hands items of clothing. At one point Joe sang the yipping cry, and he and Maria threw the things they held into the fire.

Annie's clothes, Bo realized. Maria and Joe had cared for Annie in her old age, given her a place of dignity in a trailer on the reservation above San Diego. Now they were releasing that responsibility with Annie's spirit, into another realm. But what would Bo release?

A tug at her jacket revealed a young girl, a budding teenager with flowers braided in her dark hair.

"I am Paintbrush," the girl whispered proudly, "great-granddaughter of Sees the Dark, who died to save you. Here." She placed something, a skirt, in Bo's hand, and backed away. A full corduroy skirt like one Bo had worn in junior high school. Stained now, with Annie Garcia's blood.

Bo held the garment against her stomach and wept. Beside her a small, frizzy head bobbed and lurched in the slow rhythm of the dance. And the chant wound its way through her, endlessly repeating, until her feet, the others, the fire, the ground, were one thing in a moment with no beginning and no end. Just there, outside of time.

Laurie was in that moment, Bo sensed. Peaceful and fond as a night breeze.

Somehow, it was over.

"Aiyee-ip!" The sound rose up and escaped Bo's lips without her awareness as she threw Annie's garment into the fire.

It was over.

Taking the child's hand, she turned to walk slowly away from the fire, toward Estrella and Andrew LaMarche.

A deaf child would live, and so would she.

It was, really, over.